THE
LAST GOOD DAY

THE
LAST GOOD DAY

JOHN L. LANSDALE

BOOKVOICE PUBLISHING 2021

THE LAST GOOD DAY © Copyright 2021
by John L. Lansdale
All rights reserved.

Cover art © Copyright 2021
by Dirk Berger
All rights reserved.

Book design © Copyright 2021
by BookVoice Publishing
All rights reserved.

ISBN
978-1-949381-24-5 Hardcover
978-1-949381-27-6 eBook

BookVoice Publishing
PO Box 1528
Chandler, TX 75758
www.bookvoicepublishing.com

THE MECANA SERIES by John L. Lansdale
#1 - Horse of a Different Color
#2 - When the Night Bird Sings
#3 - Twisted Justice
#4 – The Box

OTHER WORKS BY JOHN L. LANSDALE
Slow Bullet
Long Walk Home
Zombie Gold
The Last Good Day
Broken Moon
Kissing the Devil
Shadows West (with Joe R. Lansdale)
Hell's Bounty (with Joe R. Lansdale)
Boy and Hog (Short Story)
Boy and Hog Return (Short Story)
Emergency Christmas (Short Story)
Tales from the Crypt (Comic Series)
That Hellbound Train (Graphic Novel)
Yours Truly, Jack the Ripper (Graphic Novel)
Shadow Warrior (Graphic Novel)
Justin Case (Graphic Novel)

What Others are Saying about John L. Lansdale

"Mickey Spillane fans will welcome this page-turner...Lansdale effectively delays revealing the novel's big secret until the end. Those who like their thrillers with a heavy dose of violent action will be satisfied." - **Publishers Weekly review of** *Slow Bullet*

"This is an entertaining, science fiction-historical-horror blend with resourceful protagonists and a solid cast of secondary characters."
- **Booklist review of** *Zombie Gold*

"*Slow Bullet* is a straight-ahead thriller...it's about action, and there's plenty of that. Check it out." - **Bill Crider's Pop Culture Magazine**

"...the author's innate ability to spin a complex tale painted with vivid characters and intense suspense provides readers with a well-paced book that they may find difficult to set down...a worthwhile suspenseful ride." - **Amazing Stories review of** *Horse of a Different Color*

"Has something for everyone... It's exciting, entertaining and educational. A fun ride." – **legendary TV personality/actress/author Joan Hallmark, review of** *Zombie Gold*

"...something unique and comfortable and difficult to put down. Highly recommended." – **Cemetery Dance review of** *Hell's Bounty*

"True to Lansdale tradition, John L. Lansdale has compiled a piece of work that should appeal to a wide range of readers."
– **Amazing Stories review of** *Zombie Gold*

"*Long Walk Home* really touched and gripped me. A great bittersweet story of light and shadow about growing up in a time gone by. I loved it." – **author Joe R. Lansdale**

The good thing about the future is it comes one day at a time.
Abraham Lincoln

To leave footprints you have to be willing to back track occasionally.
Author

For Mason

And my long distance friend Bob for our sunset watching.

1

The bullet shattered his arm and made its exit out the back of his uniform's coat sleeve. He dropped his rifle and fell from his horse to the ground. The sound of hoof beats shook the earth.

He knew the enemy was upon him. He turned his head into the soft green grass that smelled of urine and waited for that final fatal bullet to rip into his body.

Moments later, soldiers' horses jumped over him, avoiding his crumpled form as they charged up the hill toward his regiment. He rolled over on his back, tore the front of his shirt off and wrapped his bleeding arm with his one hand. He saw the remains of his severed arm on the ground and threw up. He pulled himself to his feet with his rifle and staggered behind a nearby rock and collapsed.

That was the last thing he remembered until he woke up and realized he was in a Yankee field hospital – in a large tent with other patients missing arms and legs.

A tired-looking man with shaggy gray hair and a matching beard with a stethoscope around his neck was coming his way. He stopped at the bed and picked up the left arm stub.

"What happened to my men?" The patient said, propping himself up on his good arm.

"Hello, Major Rance Allison, you've been in and out of consciousness for three days now. As for your men, some dead and wounded, some captured. I'm Colonel Jennings, the one who treated your arm and sewed it off. You lost a lot of blood, you're lucky to be alive."

"I'm not sure I want to be," Rance said.

"The war is over, major. General Lee surrendered to General Grant at Appomattox two days ago. Here's a cable you can read if you think I'm lying."

He pulled a piece of paper out of his pocket and handed it to his patient. He looked at it and dropped it on the ground.

"You can go home," Jennings said.

"I don't have a home," Rance said. "You Yankees destroyed it and murdered my wife and daughter. By now the rest of my family is probably dead, too."

"I'm sorry. War is war."

"Killing women and children is murder, Colonel. When can I get out of here?"

"It would be best to stay for three or four more days to make sure you don't get that arm infected."

"I'd like to go now."

"Not a good idea but if that's what you want to do I'll release you."

"That's what I want."

"I'll give you some medical supplies and a bottle of whiskey to numb the pain. Bathe your arm twice a day and keep it clean and dry. I can get you some clean clothes if you don't mind wearing blue."

"I'll keep what I got for now."

"Expected that, they're giving officers a horse. The Provost Marshal's tent is right over there," he pointed at a nearby tent. "They will process you out, give you back your personal things. The physical pain will go away in time, the memories won't. Take care of that arm," Jennings said and walked away.

Rance sat up, placed his legs on the floor and slowly pulled on his pants with his one hand, stuffed his night shirt into his pants and buckled his belt with some difficulty. He propped his right boot against the bed and pushed his foot into the boot, then did the same with the left and stood up. He leaned against a table to keep his balance and slipped on his tattered uniform coat with a major's insignia sewed onto the shoulder pads.

Something had happened to his hat so he brushed his fingers through his thick black hair several times to smooth it down and made a scoop with his good hand in a wash bowl and splashed water on his face and beard. A nurse brought him a small bag with a shoulder strap and he hung it over his shoulder. The other patients were staring at him. He was definitely out of place wearing a ragged blood-stained Confederate uniform in a Yankee hospital.

He made his way to the Provost Marshal's tent and went in. A big burly man with a red beard and sergeant stripes on his sleeve was packing rifles in a crate.

"The doctor said the war was over and I can leave."

"We kicked your ass," the sergeant said.

"He said I could get a horse and my personals here."

"Yeah, for some reason they wanted to save your ass. Don't know why. The only good Reb is a dead one."

"Why don't you just shut up and give me my things."

"I'd rather shoot you," the sergeant said. "But then I'd have to clean up the place. You have to sign an allegiance form to the Union before you can get a receipt for your things."

"It don't matter now. Give them to me."

The sergeant handed him the allegiance form, receipt and a pencil, and he signed them. The sergeant reached in a cabinet and picked up a small box with Major Rance Allison on the outside.

"This is all we found on you. Officers get their side arms if they had one. You didn't." He opened the box and took out a picture, a battle order and a letter. "That your wife and kid?"

"Was," Rance said. "I had a gold watch my grandpa gave me with my name on it. Where is it?"

"Don't know anything about that."

"You expect me to believe that?" Rance asked.

The sergeant stared at him for a second, shook his head no. "I didn't get it, you must've lost it on the battlefield."

"Maybe," Rance said.

"You can pick a horse out of the ones we captured. There's a sign on the gate says 'rebel horses.' Had to shoot the ones that were wounded, was harder than shooting Johnny Rebs."

"What about a saddle?"

"Don't get a saddle. You're lucky to be getting a horse. If it was me, I would let you walk home."

Rance put the picture and letter in his coat pocket, crumbled up the battle order and dropped it on the ground and walked out.

As he approached the corral he saw his buckskin. He was still alive and well. He walked up to the gate and called to him.

"Buck, come here," he said and whistled.

The horse turned toward him, shook his head and trotted over to the gate and rubbed his nose on the major's coat.

"Missed you, fella," he said and patted the horse on the neck. The horse had a bridle on, with the reins folded and tied to the bridle. He pulled them loose and lifted them over the horse's head and led him out the gate and closed it. He hung the first-aid bag around the horse's neck, grabbed a handful of his long black mane with his right hand, lifted the stub of his left arm over his back and pulled himself up.

Doctor Jennings appeared and held out a twenty-dollar gold piece for him to take.

"I don't want your money," Rance said.

"Don't be stupid. Take it, you have to eat. I overheard you in the tent. I'm sorry about your wife and daughter. I lost my wife in the war, too. She was a nurse at Gettysburg. We don't have to be enemies anymore."

Rance reached down and took the gold piece. "Thanks," he said. "What you going to do now, doc?"

"Stay in the army, I guess. They still need doctors."

"I'm sorry about your wife," Rance said.

Doctor Jennings nodded. "If I was you, I would get out of that confederate uniform soon as I could," he said and walked away.

It was a bright and clear day under a high blue sky as Rance rode out. A rumbling wind whistled through the leaves on the cottonwood trees and blew the lingering smell of death across the silent battlefield as he rode away from the camp.

He wasn't sure he wanted to go home. The pain was not just in his arm. Everything he loved was gone.

2

Hours later he stopped at a small winding creek, laid the medical bag on the bank and waded into the creek up to his waist to sooth his horse-sore ass while Buck drank.

As he stood there, a red robin flew to a tree on the edge of the creek. Then another, both perched on a limb overhanging the creek, chirping at each other. No sounds of cannons or gunfire for the first time in four years. The war was really over.

Rance got out of the creek, picked up the bag and led Buck to a large rock to climb on. He heard hoof beats and saw three riders atop a nearby hill, coming his way at a full gallop. There was no way he could outrun them riding bareback with one hand. He drew Buck close and waited.

Two men wearing dirty Confederate uniforms rode in leading a third. The birds flew away. One was a sergeant, the other one a corporal leading the third rider's horse. The third man was wearing a Union uniform, his hands tied to the saddle horn and a bandana muzzled in his mouth. They pulled their horses up and got off, leaving the other man on his horse. The sergeant hanging on to the reins.

"Where you headed, major?" the sergeant asked.

"On my way home," Rance said.

"Where's that?"

"Milberg. In the Shenandoah Valley."

"Kinda messed you up, didn't they," the corporal said, pointing to Rance's missing arm. "We'll get even for you with this blue belly."

The sergeant was tall and thin with a crooked nose and a salt-and-pepper beard. He had a Navy-issued Colt stuck in his belt. The corporal was smaller with shaggy brown hair, cold blue eyes and several days of black stubble on his face. He had a Bowie knife strapped to his belt and a brass spyglass lopped on his saddle horn.

The rider in the Union uniform was an Indian with long black braided hair to his waist and a black feather stuck in the band of his hat, his face bruised and swollen, sitting a solid black horse.

"Do you know the war's over? Lee surrendered," Rance said.

"We heard that," the sergeant said. "We decided to quit some time back."

"You're deserters?"

"Not anymore," the sergeant said and grinned. "You can call me Jake and this is Smiley. What's your name, major sir?"

"Rance Allison. Why don't you let the Indian go?"

"Can't do that, major, we're going to scalp him," Smiley said. "The trading post will give us fifty dollars in gold for a Indian scalp. But we're having trouble deciding if we want to hang him then scalp him, or scalp him then hang him." Smiley and Jake both laughed.

"Don't think that's a good idea either way," Rance said. "Cut him loose."

"We don't care what you think," Smiley said. "Don't take orders no more."

Rance watched as the Indian franticly pulled on the ropes that bound him behind the soldiers.

"You got any gold or Yankee money, major?" Jake asked.

Rance lied. "No," he said, knowing he had the twenty-dollar gold piece in his pocket.

"What's in that bag hanging on the horse's neck?" the corporal asked.

"Medical supplies for my arm."

"Let me see," the sergeant said and snatched the bag off Buck, jerking his head back. He opened the bag, dumped the contents on the ground and spotted a half-pint of whiskey.

"Well looky here," he said and picked up the bottle. "What's this?"

"For the pain," Rance said.

"Looks like you been easing your pain some," Jake said, shaking the bottle. He opened the bottle, took a big gulp and handed it to the corporal, who drank what was left then threw the bottle in the creek.

The Indian pulled his hands free, jerked the bandana out of his mouth and dove off his horse, knocking Jake to the ground, the Colt flying from his belt landing several feet away. Smiley drew his knife and started swinging it at the Indian. The Indian grabbed Smiley's wrist and they fell to the ground, wrestling for the knife. Jake got to his feet looking for the Colt. Rance beat him to it, cocked and fired.

Jake staggered forward a couple feet and fell dead.

The Indian twisted the knife from Smiley's hand, grabbed him by the collar and cut his throat from ear to ear.

Rance pointed the Colt at the Indian and cocked it.

"Don't shoot! I'm done," he said, dropping the bloody knife on the ground.

Rance lowered the Colt and looked at his bleeding left arm. The bandage was torn loose and a stitch had come out.

"You better do something about that arm, major, before you bleed to death."

Rance took a couple of steps back, reached down and picked up the bandage and iodine off the ground while hanging on to the Colt.

"You won't be able to do that with one hand holding that Colt," the Indian said.

"I'll manage. Stay where you are," Rance said.

Blood was running from the stub of his arm at a faster pace. He blinked his eyes and saw two Indians. He dropped the Colt and fell to the ground, out cold.

Sometime later, he woke up with his arm bandaged, his head lying on his bag. He saw the Indian sitting by a small fire, the sergeant's Colt in his belt. A rabbit was roasting on a stick over the fire, the two dead Confederates lying where they fell.

Rance rose up on his good arm. "How come you're still here?" he asked.

"Was getting hungry, figured I would eat and wait to see if I needed to bury you."

"Why?" Rance said.

"You kept that bastard from shooting me, figured I owed you something for that. Want some rabbit?"

"Yeah, think I do," Rance said. "Thanks for bandaging my arm."

The Indian cut a piece of the rabbit off with Smiley's knife and brought it to him then went back to the fire and sat down. Rance hadn't noticed before how big the man was. He was over six foot and the Indian was half a head taller.

"Where did you learn to speak English?" Rance asked.

"My mama and missionary school. That a surprise to you?"

"It is. Your mama not Indian?"

"No, a colored slave. Not sure who my daddy was except he was Indian. Don't think she knew either. Was passed around to a lot of bucks."

"What tribe?"

"Cherokee," he said. "North Carolina."

"Got a name?"

"Gv-nah-ge Tadewi."

"What's that mean?"

"Black Wind."

"Noticed you was darker than most Cherokees. The Cherokee in that region had slaves, fought for the Confederacy. How come you didn't?"

"Had a different feeling bout it," he said. "Better eat your rabbit, major, it's getting cold."

Rance nodded and took a bite.

"Where's home, major?" Black Wind said.

"The Shenandoah Valley. A little town called Milberg."

"My misguided Cherokee brothers fought some battles in the valley under General Early."

"I know," Rance said. "Your mama still with the tribe?"

"She died from the fever last year. She was traded to the Cherokee for a horse. We belonged to Chief Yo-nu-gv-ya-s-gi, that's Drowning Bear to you white folks. The chief was considered a prophet. Was supposed to have died, went to heaven and came back. I barely remember him. He died for good when I was little. Probably was too old to be my papa but he was big as me, maybe? What bout you, major, you have slaves?"

"No, never did."

"Then why you wearing that uniform?"

"Like you, I have my reasons."

"You do know what the war was bout?" Black Wind said.

"It was more than freeing the slaves," Rance said. "They wanted our land and control of the southern states."

"Not sure I buy that. I think you made the wrong decision. But...you paid for it and we won the war. I'll settle for that. Let bygones be bygones. No sense in us hating each other anymore."

"What about them," Rance said, looking at the dead men.

"Got no forgiveness for them."

"How did they get the drop on you?" Rance asked. "You're big enough to go bear hunting with a switch."

"Stupid for the most part," he said. "Got drunk and wound up in a place I shouldn't have been, and the next thing I know I'm tied to my horse with those two idiots telling me they're going to scalp me and sell my hair to a renegade trader."

"Where you headed now?"

"Can't go back home, they would scalp me. We can ride along together while I think it over and watch each other's back. Or go our separate ways, not opposed to either one."

"Might be better to ride together for now till some of the hostility on both sides wears down a bit," Rance said.

"That's goin' to be a long time." Black Wind walked over to the two dead men, emptied their pockets, grabbed them by their collars with each hand, dragged them to the creek and rolled them in. He untied the horses, reached in Jake's saddle bags and took out two small sacks. "Heavy. Let's see what we got here." He placed the sacks on a rock and untied the sacks and looked in. "Full of gold and silver coins," he said. "Must be over two hundred dollars here. Looks like they been outlawin.' I'll split it with you."

"Don't want it," Rance said, struggling to get to his feet.

"Then I'll keep it." He reached in Smiley's saddle bag and took out a tomahawk. "Almost forgot that bastard had my tomahawk," he said and stuck the tomahawk in his belt. "They both got Henry's in their saddle boots. Best we move on fore we need them. You can saddle your horse later with one of their saddles."

He handed the reins to Smiley's horse to Rance. He hesitated for a moment then took the reins.

The two men gave each other a long look before mounting. They knew there was more to be said but it could wait. Rance pulled himself up on Smiley's horse and looped Buck's reins over the brass spyglass on the saddle horn .

"Wish we had killed them fore they drank the whiskey," Black Wind said.

"You got a Christian name?" Rance asked.

"B.W. Ramsey. Ramsey was my mama's slave name. Indians called her Dark Sky. Got no problem with B.W. I'll just call you major."

Rance nodded okay.

3

They rode along in silence most of the day, each holding his thoughts before Rance spoke.

"We're getting close to a town called Whiskey Gulch if I remember right. Maybe we can get a bath and some clean clothes there."

"You do stink," B.W. said.

"And you don't?" Rance said.

"Naw. Indians have a kind of tree bark smell, blends in."

"Bullshit."

"It's a fact. My mama said we did and white people smell like lattice."

"Lattice doesn't have a smell."

"Does to us."

Rance shook his head.

As they topped the next hill, Whiskey Gulch came into view – a one street mining town with three or four saloons, a livery stable and a mercantile store.

It was dusk when they rode in, the only light coming from the saloons. A lady from the balcony of a two-story saloon waved a lace handkerchief at them and pulled her skirt up to show her leg and smiled as they rode by.

Most of the horses tied to the hitching post along the street looked like plow horses instead of cow ponies

A two-horse wagon with "Caraway Mines" painted on the side of the wagon was tied to a hitching post in front of a saloon. A sign in the window read: Hot baths $5.

"Looks like we hit town 'bout the same time all the miners did," Rance said.

"Maybe we should get us a drink, something to eat and move on," B.W. said.

"I'm goin' to get me a hot bath with soap and clean clothes," Rance said.

"Think I'll wait," B.W. said.

Two men staggered out of the saloon, one falling into B.W.'s horse. B.W. kicked him away and he staggered on down the street.

"Trust me, you don't smell like a tree," Rance said."Well, at least not a live one."

"You go ahead," B.W. said. "I'll take the horses to the livery stable. Don't think I want to pay five dollars for a bath anyway. You got money?"

Rance nodded.

"I'll come back and buy you a drink," B.W. said.

"Suit yourself," Rance said, dismounted and handed B.W. the reins to Smiley's horse and to Buck, then walked in the saloon.

B.W. sat there on his horse for a moment, looking at the swinging doors, inhaling the whiskey smell that drifted into the street. He wiped his mouth like he could taste the whiskey and led the horses to the livery stable.

A young boy dressed in overalls, barefooted with shaggy blonde hair and bright blue eyes was sweeping out stalls.

"Can I get some feed and water for my horses?" B.W. asked.

"Yes sir," the boy said. "Fifty cents a horse."

"That grain and hay?"

"Yes sir," the boy said.

"Alright. Here's two dollars." B.W. handed him two one-dollar gold pieces. "Unsaddle them and put the saddles back on after they eat. Put the saddle on the bay on the buckskin. I'll be back in a couple of hours and those rifles better still be on the saddles."

A big man with a grisly face and a long black beard walked in chewing on a chicken leg. "I'll take that," he said, slapped the boy and held out his stubby-fingered hand for the money. The boy rubbed his jaw and dropped the money in his hand and led the horses to the stalls.

"No need for that," B.W. said.

"Mind your own business, Injun."

"You his papa?" B.W. asked.

"No. He just hangs around, helps out a little. I feed him and let him sleep in the stable. Tries to steal my money every chance he gets."

"Don't have a mama?" B.W. asked.

"Mama was a whore. A cowboy shot her couple years ago for stealin' his money."

"They catch him?"

"Didn't try. Don't nobody care what happens to whores."

"What about his papa?"

"Ain't answerin' no more questions."

The boy walked up. He couldn't have been more than ten or twelve. "I took care of them, Mr. Harden," the boy said.

Harden gave the boy an angry look and looked back at B.W. "If you don't come back for them tonight it will cost you more money."

"Be back tonight," B.W. said.

Harden checked the money, put it in his pocket and walked away.

When B.W. went in the saloon, four big men with straggly beards and thick muscular bodies wearing coal dust overalls were holding Rance against the bar. Two of the men were hanging on his good arm, one holding the bad arm, and the other one with a handful of his hair, tilting his head back and pouring whiskey down his gullet. Several other men were standing back from the bar with whiskey glasses in their hands, yelling, "More! More! More!" A bald-headed bartender was leaning on the bar with a smile on his face and two young whores were holding the piano player's head back, mocking the scene.

"Let him go," B.W. said.

The one pouring the whiskey stopped pouring and stepped in front of Rance, holding the bottle.

"What's that you said there, chief?"

"I said, let him go."

"This Johnnie Reb wanted a drink," he said and everyone laughed.

"War's over, let him go," B.W. said.

The other men were still hanging on to Rance.

"Figured you would enjoy this considerin' the uniform you wearin,'" the one with the bottle said.

"You okay, major?" B.W. asked.

"Kinda woozy," Rance said.

Everybody laughed. The whores let go of the piano player and joined the laughter.

"For the last time, let him go," B.W. said.

"And if we don't?" the man with the bottle said.

"Then I'll have to insist."

Everyone laughed again.

"How you goin' to do that? You're kind of outnumbered," the man with the bottle said, prompting another round of laughter.

"You'll be the first to know," B.W. said and eased his right hand under the handle of his tomahawk.

The man waved the bottle at B.W. "Got no more patience with you, chief," he said and reached for a .44 on his hip. It was the last thing he would ever do.

B.W. gave a heave upward to the handle of his tomahawk, grabbed it in midair and hurled it across the room, splitting the man's skull. His gun hand fell away from the gun The whiskey bottle fell from his other hand and they both crashed to the floor.

B.W. drew his Colt, pointed it at the men holding Rance and they let go and backed off.

"I'll shoot the first one goes for a gun," B.W. said.

Everyone looked at the dead man as his blood pooled around him on the floor. Nobody moved.

"Think that bath's going to have to wait," B.W. said.

"Think so too." Rance turned his head, squinting his eyes trying to focus on the man on the floor.

He pulled the .44 from the dead man's holster, stuck it under his left arm and pried the tomahawk out of the man's bleeding skull and pitched it to B.W. He pulled the pistol from under his left arm with his right hand and pointed it at the crowd as they backed out of the saloon and ran for the livery stable.

Several of the men from the saloon ran out on the street, shooting at them. When they ran in the stable the stable boy was holding their horses saddled, waiting for them.

"You better get out of here quick," he said.

"Thanks," B.W. said. "You want to go with us?"

"Let me get my things," he said.

"We don't have time," Rance said but the boy ran to a hay stack anyway and pulled out a small feed sack and ran back to the horses.

"I'm ready," the boy said.

"Get on the roan," B.W. said.

"We can't take the boy with us," Rance said, looked at the saddle on Buck, grabbed the saddle horn and swung up in the saddle. "Where did we get another saddle?"

"I stole it," the boy said. "Well, Harden stole it first."

"You can't go," Rance said.

"He has to now," B.W. said.

"Damn," Rance said. "All I wanted was a bath."

The sound of angry people was almost to the livery. The boy and B.W. mounted and Harden came running in, buttoning his pants.

"What the hell you doing," he said. "Where you takin' that boy?"

B.W. spurred his horse and galloped toward the blacksmith, kicked him in the chest as he rode by, knocking him down. They rode into the night with bullets whizzing past them.

4

They rode hard by the light of a full moon until they felt the miners had given up the chase.

Rance slowed Buck to a walk and B.W. and the boy brought their horses to him.

"Okay, explain," Rance said.

"Bout the boy?" B.W. asked.

"Of course 'bout the boy."

"Don't have no kin, was being beat on by that blacksmith. Had to get him out of there."

"That'll do for me. What's your name boy?" Rance asked.

"Thomas Travers," he said. "Call me Tommy."

"You set a horse real good, Tommy," Rance said.

"Thank you."

"I owe you for your help back there, B.W.," Rance said.

"Makes us even. You on your own next time though," B.W. said.

"Fair enough," Rance said. "We need to get out of these uniforms."

"And get the boy some shoes," B.W. said.

"And me and you a new hat," Rance said and grinned.

"I need a hat too," Tommy said. "I can buy my own. I got five dollars I swiped from Mr. Harden."

"That's the kind of talk that would have got me a serious whipping when I was a boy, Tommy" Rance said. "But considerin,' I think he owed you that. Right, B.W.?"

"Right," B.W. said. "You still drunk?"

"Pretty well wore off now. A couple hours of sleep wouldn't hurt."

"I'm for that," B.W. said. "How 'bout you, Tommy, you bushed?"

"Pretty much."

"How old are you boy?" B.W. asked.

"Twelve, I think. Not real sure."

"Was your mama murdered?"

"Yeah, how did you know?"

"The blacksmith said something about it."

"I don't want to talk about it anymore," Tommy said.

"Okay," B.W. said.

They rode into a clump of trees and dismounted.

"I'll unsaddle the horses," Tommy said.

"That's right kind of you boy," Rance said as Tommy led the horses to a low-hanging tree limb.

Next morning, Rance was having trouble tightening the girth on his saddle. Tommy ran over and grabbed the girth to help.

"I can do it, boy, don't need your help."

Tommy turned the girth loose and Rance continued wrestling with it.

"Boy was just trying to help, major," B.W. said.

"Don't need no help."

"Yes you do," B.W. said. "Me or the boy can tighten that for you, or you can be stubborn and take forever to do it. Which is it?"

Rance stopped pulling and dropped his head. "Yeah, go ahead," he said and backed away from his horse. "Not much of a man anymore."

"You'll have to do some things different now, that's all," B.W. said.

Rance didn't say anything and waited for B.W. to tighten the girth and climbed on his horse. They rode a ways and saw buzzards circling in the distance.

"Want to have a look?" Rance asked.

"Might as well," B.W. said.

They came to a burned-out house and barn. Buzzards were swarming the half-eaten carcasses of a horse in a corral with what looked like two bullet holes in his neck.

"Think it was Indians?" Rance asked.

"No," B.W. said. "They would have stolen that horse, to ride or eat. Don't see any bodies."

"Not much of anything, really," Rance said. "Everything's burnt to a crisp."

"There's wagon tracks and hoof prints leadin' out of here," B.W. said. "Must have made a run for it."

Tommy came running up, carrying three jars of canned peaches. "Look what I found in the cellar. There's more if we want them."

"Good job, boy," B.W. said. "I'm starving."

"Me too," Rance said.

"May taste better if we move over the hill to get away from the smell," B.W. said.

"Yeah," Tommy said and handed Rance and B.W. a jar of peaches. "I'll get the horses."

"Well one thing you gotta say for that boy, he's helpful," B.W. said.

"He is," Rance said.

Tommy led the horses over the hill and Rance and B.W. followed and sat down under a big oak and the wind picked up the smell.

"Well I guess we eat with the stench or don't eat at all," Rance said.

"After the last four years ain't nothin' much gets in the way of me eatin' when I'm hungry," B.W. said.

"Yeah, me too," Rance said.

"What you goin' to do when you get to the valley, major?" B.W. asked.

"Not sure. The Union commandeered our land that's been in the family for over a hundred years, don't think I can get it back. Mainly just wanted to visit my wife and daughter's graves, didn't get a chance to bury anyone else. What about you?"

"Thought about practicin' law. The tribe sent me to law school with the help of a white man named William Holland Thomas. He became chief after Drowning Bear died. Only white man to ever be chief of the Cherokee. He thought the tribe needed an Indian representin' them. For all I know he could have been my papa. I may not even be an Indian."

"Heard of him. Led the Cherokee against the Union," Rance said. " I'll say one thing for him – he never lost a battle to Union troops. Probably should have been leading the Confederacy instead of Lee."

"Lee was so impressed with himself he didn't think he could lose," B.W. said.

"How come you didn't have any rank with an education like you have," Rance said.

"Didn't want any. Didn't tell them about the schoolin' or the colored part. Tried to make me a sergeant a couple of times when they found out I could read and write but I turned it down. Didn't waste no time getting rid of me when the war was over."

"I went to West Point," Rance said. "Kind of the same thing in reverse. Was fighting Apaches when the war broke out. By the time I got home it was too late, everyone was dead. The Yankees hung my papa from his front porch and burned the house down around him and my mama. Nothin' left of them to bury. Murdered my wife and daughter as they ran away. My neighbor Julie and her family found them and buried them for me. Had two brothers killed fightin' for the union in '61. Don't know where they are. Resigned my commission when I got a letter from Julie telling me what happened at home. Paid a visit to my wife. Spent some time there grieving and joined the Confederates. We never owned any slaves and my pa hadn't fired a shot against no one. No need for what they did, no need at all. Destroyed our farms and slaughtered our families because they could."

B.W. stared off into the distance studying the soft white clouds, wrinkling his nose at the smell, eating his peaches. "Sorry 'bout your family," he said. "Only one I had was my mama. I liked being an Indian. Now I can't go back. Seams we both have good reasons for what we did. If you look at our point of view."

"Did what I thought I had to do at the time," Rance said.

"I had a good reason for what I did. Me and Mama was slaves," B.W. said, digging in the can of peaches with his knife "Theses peaches are good but the stench is so strong it smells like the whole world has been skunked."

"I know who my papa is," Tommy said.

"You do?" B.W. said surprised.

"His name is Robert Travers from Texas," Tommy said. "My mama told me all about him. He owns a railroad. Told everybody after my mama died but they laughed at me, said I was making up a story."

"Are you?" Rance asked.

"No, it's true. I got a letter to prove it. It's in my stash. I'll show you."

Tommy jumped up and ran to his horse and untied the gunny sack.

"Sounds like his mama fixed up a pretty important papa for him," B.W. said.

"Yeah, owns a railroad," Rance said.

Tommy came running back to Rance and B.W., sat down and untied his sack and picked up a faded letter and a picture from the sack. "I tried to show this to everyone but no one would read it." He handed the letter and picture to Rance.

"Can you read, Tommy ?" Rance asked.

"No, but my mama could. She read it to me a lot. I know every word of it."

Rance glanced at the picture, then the letter. It was hand written on Travers Southern Railway – Traversville, Texas letterhead dated 15 July 1853 to Alice Woodson c/o Big Sally's Saloon.

Rance read the letter aloud, Tommy lip-synching the words.

"My dear Alice, I'm sorry to inform you that I cannot continue to see you. I am enclosing a hundred dollars and a train ticket to Whiskey Gulch, Virginia where you and Tommy can stay on my cousin's farm for as long as you like. His name is Billy Freeman. He is expecting you. I will send fifty dollars every month for your future care. I have no other choice. My father said because of your past I have to break all ties or he will disinherit me. If you do not accept this arrangement then I will deny any kind of relationship ever existed and have no further contact with you or the boy. I hope you will accept my offer. Signed, Robert Travers."

Rance looked at the picture and handed it to B.W. The man in the picture was tall, good-looking, maybe in his thirties, well-dressed in a suit with a watch chain hanging out of a vest pocket. He had on a bowler hat with thick hair sticking out from it. A pretty young lady was standing beside him holding an infant.

"Where did your mama get the name Thomas?" Rance asked. "Shouldn't it be Robert if that's your daddy?"

"Was my mama's daddy's name. He was killed by Indians," Tommy said.

"Do you know if Robert ever sent your mama money?" Rance asked.

"Some," Tommy said. "Mama said Billy was keeping it. We stayed with Billy until the war started. He learned me how to ride and shoot then got himself killed by some Union soldiers for being a Confederate. Then me and mama had to leave and she got a job at the saloon."

"This may be your papa, Tommy," B.W. said, "but it looks like he didn't want to see you or your mama anymore, why he sent you away."

Tommy snatched the letter and picture from B.W., jumped up and stuck them in the sack. "I know she was a whore. I'm old enough to know what that is. The picture was when I was born. At least I know who my papa was. That's more than you do." He ran to his horse, tied the sack back on the saddle and took off at a hard gallop.

"Where you goin', boy?" Rance yelled. But he kept riding and disappeared over the next rise.

"Didn't handle that very well, did I?" B.W. said.

"Nope," Rance said. "Let's go get him."

They mounted and saw a flock of buzzards filling the sky from over the rise. Just before they toped the hill Tommy appeared, riding as fast as he could towards them.

"What the hell?" B.W. said. "What's that boy doin?'"

Tommy reined down his horse beside them and wheeled him around. "Come with me," he said and took off in a hard gallop.

"Tommy come back here!" Rance yelled, but he kept riding.

B.W. and Rance spurred their horses after Tommy. When they topped the rise, Tommy was sitting on his horse in front of a big oak tree. A colored man and a boy, about Tommy's age, were hanging from the tree, naked. Their eyes were gone, loose, stringy flesh hanging from all parts of their bodies. A note was pinned on an overturned wagon. "What free niggers get." Big chunks of meat were tore out of the wagon's two dead horses still in harnesses.

They sat motionless on their horses, trying to absorb the reality of what they were seeing. Tommy threw up his peaches.

B.W. drew his knife, rode up to them holding one hand over his mouth and cut them down. "Maybe there's a shovel in the wagon." He dismounted and led his horse to the wagon. He saw a pair of stained leather gloves in the wagon. He picked up the gloves and walked over to the man and laid a glove over his hand. It was way too small for him. B.W. saw a paper blowing by, stepped on it and picked it up. It was a receipt for ten pounds of flour made out to Leon Brookings from Catching's Trading Post. He stuck the receipt in his pocket and put the gloves in his saddle bags.

"Wasn't no tools in the wagon," he said.

"We'll figure out somethin,'" Rance said.

"Still think you were on the right side, major?"

"Don't know how to answer that."

"Would think there would be a woman around with the boy but ain't seen nothin' to say that."

"Was thinking the same thing," Rance said. "May have taken her with them."

"You know what that means," B.W. said.

"Yeah, I'm afraid so," Rance said.

B.W. mounted and rode over to Tommy. "I'm sorry for what I said back there."

"Don't seem that important anymore," Tommy said. "Don't know why I even kept that letter. We goin' to look for the ones that did this?"

"Don't know yet," B.W. said.

B.W. showed Rance the name on the receipt. "Ever hear of that place?"

"Not too far from here," Rance said.

They found a depression deep enough for the bodies and covered them with rocks. B.W. scratched "Brookings Family" on a big rock near them and they rode away.

5

After a half-hour ride from the Brookings place, a dark cloud blew in from the west and it started to rain. They found an overhang from a ledge that kept them from getting soaked and waited for the rain to stop.

When the sun came back out, they rode on for a mile or two, topped a ridge and saw a long clapboard building no more than fifty yards away beside a small railroad depot that was boarded up, and a railroad water tower shot full of holes. A cattle car with "Travers Southern Railway" on it was sitting on the tracks beside the water tower.

"Look at that," B.W. said. Rance shook his head. B.W. returned it with a nod and didn't say anything else. They rode up to the hitching post.

Two horses were tied to the hitching post hooked to a wagon in front. One of the horses was sitting on his butt.

They dismounted and tied their horses next to the wagon. The trough in front of the horses was dry. A sign over the door said "Catching's Trading Post."

"Them horses look like they're about to keel over," Rance said.

"Want me to see if I can find some feed and water?" Tommy asked.

"Let's check it out first," B.W. said and pulled his rifle out of the saddle boot and cocked it. "I'll go in first. Tommy, you stay behind the major."

The place had been ransacked. All kinds of goods, clothes, farm equipment and feed were scattered all over the floor. Mirrors were shattered and canned-good shelves pulled down.

"Hello," he said. "Anybody here?" No one answered. "Hello," he said again. Nothing.

Rance and Tommy walked up beside him, looking at the mess. "Wow," Tommy said, "Somebody really tore this place up."

"Should be a well around here somewhere," B.W. said. "Tommy, see if you can get those horses a couple of buckets of water and some feed. We'll take care of ours later." Tommy nodded and hurried outside.

Rance looked around the room and noticed a boot sticking out from an overturned shelf. "Look there," he said, gesturing toward the boot. They raised the shelf up and a skinny old man with a wrinkled face, white hair and a long white beard was lying on his back with two dried-blood bullet holes in his plaid shirt.

"Looks like he's been dead for a while. Maybe about the time the Brookings were hung," Rance said.

"Most likely the same ones did both," B.W. said. "That Catching's?"

"Never been in here," Rance said.

B.W. searched the dead man's pockets and came up with a wallet, removed several Union bills from it and stuck them in his pocket, then unfolded a paper and looked at it. "That's him," he said.

"You were supposed to be finding out who he was, not robbing him," Rance said.

"We'll pay him back by burying him," B.W. said.

"That's right Christian of you. Maybe you did learn something at that missionary school."

"I'll dig the grave since you're kind of at a disadvantage."

"How many you think did this?" Rance said.

"Hard to tell. Looks like a lot of hoof prints out there. Rain messed them up some, maybe three or four headed south. Might go lookin' for them if it wasn't for the boy."

"That does pose a problem," Rance said. "You think his papa really owns the railroad?"

"Name's on that cattle car but if he is, Tommy was an accident," B.W. said. "Travers couldn't marry a whore so he got rid of them. Didn't even have the guts to tell them face to face."

"Feel bad for the boy," Rance said.

"Why I'm holdin' off goin' after them varmints," B.W. said. "Don't want any harm to come to him."

Tommy walked back in. "I got the horses out of their harness, watered and fed them. There's a lean-to out back with a place for the horses and a stove and tub for that bath you wanted, major."

"Think we got time for a bath, B.W., or do you still think you smell like a tree?"

"What's he talkin' 'bout?" Tommy asked.

"He don't know," B.W. said.

"I don't take baths," Tommy said.

"You do now," Rance said.

"Why do we have to take a bath?" Tommy said. "We ain't goin' to church or nothin.'"

"Beats me," B.W. said. "Got this on his mind and won't let it go. Might as well get it over with."

"I'll start a fire, heat some water and take care of the animals," Rance said. "B.W., you and the boy look for some clothes and somethin' to eat."

B.W. and Tommy looked at each other and shook their heads.

"You could shoot him, B.W.," Tommy said.

"Been considerin' that."

"See if there are any weapons around," Rance said. "We may need all the firepower we can get."

"Been considerin' that too," B.W. said.

"Thinks he's still in the army givin' orders," Tommy said. B.W. grinned.

By the time they got their baths, Rance shaved his beard and they changed clothes and fed themselves and the animals, it was getting dark. Rance found a lamp and lit it.

"Looks like the rain's coming back. Might as well stay here for the night and ride out in the morning."

"Think so too," B.W. said. "Get some sleep. I'll take the first watch. Wake you when I get tired. How's the arm?"

"Hurts some but I can handle it."

"Need whiskey 'bout now?" B.W. said.

"Me or you?" Rance asked.

"Both."

"Might better load that shotgun you found."

"Was going to do that," B.W. said and pointed a finger at Tommy.

He had fallen asleep on a pile of clothes in a corner wearing his new boots with a peppermint stick in his hand.

"Long day," Rance said.

"You ever been to Texas, major?"

"No."

"Me neither. Think Travers is still alive?"

"No telling."

"No matter, it would be his estate that's liable regardless," B.W. said.

"Yeah, kind of leaves us with a choice, don't it," Rance said. "Don't have nothin' else to do."

"May not do any good," B.W. said. "But we won't know if we don't try."

"True," Rance said. "Let's think on it. I found four bottles of whiskey in a cabinet. Put 'em in my saddle bags. Think you would know when to stop if I let you have some?"

"I'll force myself," B.W. said.

"I'll get it," Rance said.

B.W. cracked the breech of the twelve-gauge, loaded two shells, eased the barrels shut and sat down on the floor facing the front door. He laid the Henry beside his leg, leaned against a fallen shelf and placed the shotgun across his lap. Two rats ran out from behind the shelves and scampered across the floor, disappearing in a corner piled up with clothes. B.W. stuffed his pants in his boots. The roar of thunder rumbled across the sky and lightning flashed through the cracks in the walls as the rain began a steady tap on the tin roof.

Rance brought a bottle of whiskey back, sat it down beside B.W., took the cap off and handed it to B.W. He lifted the bottle to his lips, titled it back and began to sallow in big gulps. Like a baby with a milk bottle. Rance reached up and took the bottle out of his hand.

"That's it for now," Rance said and stood up with the bottle.

"That was just enough to make me want more," B.W. said.

"I could see that. Why I took it away."

"Anyone else do that I would beat the hell out of them."

"Think you could, huh? Looks like whiskey brings your temper out," Rance said and walked away.

6

The next morning, sunshine was warming a clear April sky. They filled their canteens and put canned food in their saddle bags. B.W. tied the loaded double-barrel to his saddle and put three boxes of buckshot in the saddle bags. He stuck a wooden cross in the ground on Catching's grave, removed the feather from his old hat and sat the hat on top of the cross. He placed the feather in the band of his new black hat, brushed his long braided black hair back and set the hat on his head, twisted it a little to the left, pushing it down on his head, and climbed up in the saddle.

Rance rode by the corral behind the store and opened the gate, flushing the two horses out and watched them run across a field. Tommy rode up beside him.

"Think they'll be okay?" Tommy asked.

"Be fine, they'll have plenty of grass and water out there," Rance said.

"How you like my new black hat and boots?" Tommy said, shaking his foot at Rance.

Rance pushed his new black hat back on his head. "We look like the Three Musketeers," Rance
said.

"The who?" Tommy asked.

"Never mind," Rance said. "I'll tell you later."

B.W. rode up beside Rance. "You get the whiskey, major?"

"I did," Rance said. "Belongs to me."

"You may need somethin' for the pain," B.W. said.

Rance grinned. "You might too," he said and they rode away.

A short time later, Tommy rode up beside B.W. and Rance. "I been thinkin,' where do you think them riders went after they hung the colored folks?"

"Hard to say," B.W. said. "The tracks looks like they're headed the same way we've been. Might be the ones that killed old man Catching too. But could have been anybody made them tracks."

"Suits me if they went their way and we go ours," Rance said.

"You mean you don't care that they hung those people and killed Mr. Catching?" Tommy asked.

"No, but I don't want us to be next either," Rance said. "Sometimes it's not what you do but what you don't that's the right thing."

"That right, B.W.?" Tommy said.

"Don't know," B.W. said. "Think the major is saying we should mind our own business."

"Something like that," Rance said. "Could back ourselves into a corner we can't get out of."

"Is that what you think, B.W.?" Tommy said.

"Best to let whatever happens happen. Don't worry too much about it 'fore it does," B.W. said.

"That doesn't always work," Rance said. "Need to plan before jumping in the fire. If you can't come up with a plan, don't do it. Learned that at West Point."

"Usually go by my gut feeling," B.W. said. "Been right so far."

"You been lucky," Rance said.

"Maybe."

A couple hours later, they stopped on a hill and looked down into a valley at a small town.

"What's that place?" Tommy said.

"Wheeler, I think," Rance said. "A rebel stronghold durin' the war. Union never really took control of it. This part of Virginia was mixed. Never knew who was on your side. Might be best to go around and go on to Milberg, considerin' what happened at the last place."

"What we going to do in Milberg?" Tommy said.

"The major wanted to visit his family's graves," B.W. said.

"Then what?" Tommy said.

"Then what, major?" B.W. asked.

"Don't know yet," Rance said.

"Think I hooked up with the wrong people," Tommy said.

"Probably did," B.W. said. "You can't go back, though, they'd hang you."

Tommy rubbed his neck and swallowed hard.

"Need somethin' solid to eat, like a steak," B.W. said. "Before I try to do any serious thinking."

Rance nodded in agreement.

The dirt streets had turned to a muddy mess from the rain. Two men in Confederate uniforms were thrashing around in the mud, holding a bottle in one hand and firing a pistol into the air with the other, yelling, "We got him!" Loud music and laughter were coming from the saloons. It was the middle of the afternoon.

"They're celebratin' something awful early in the day," B.W. said. "Wonder if they know they lost the war."

"We won't tell 'em," Rance said. "This Looks like one of those places you shouldn't be to me," Rance said.

B.W. nodded. "Does. Let's go in?"

"I don't think you know what you say sometimes," Rance said "Remember the last saloon we was in didn't turn out so good? And this is rebel country."

"Won't know who we are this time," B.W. said. "Hell, we don't know who we are."

B.W. and Rance dismounted and handed the reins to Tommy.

"Take the horses to the livery keep them saddled," Rance said. "We'll join you in a little while, bring you some grub."

"Ain't nothin' in there I ain't seen," Tommy said. "You just want to get me out of the way so you can get drunk and chase whores."

"Take the horses to the livery stable," B.W. said.

"I don't want to, " Tommy said.

"I know," B.W. said, "but I'm bigger than you. Do it."

Tommy led the horse's away. They walked in the saloon. The place was filled with a lot of men wearing rebel uniforms, several of them dancing with the whores as the piano player pounded out Dixie.

They walked up to the bar beside a rail-thin man wearing a rebel uniform. B.W. laid a silver dollar on the bar.

"What's all the hoopla?" Rance asked.

The man turned to Rance, smiling. "He's dead. Somebody shot that sonofabitch."

"Shot who?" Rance asked.

"Lincoln," the man said. "We got a telegram this morning. Shot him at the theater last night, died this morning.

"You hear that, B.W.?" Rance said.

"I heard," he said. B.W. looked at the man. "Are they sure?"

"Yep, he's dead alright." He turned back to the bar and held his glass up for more whiskey.

"Might be time to go," Rance said. B.W. didn't answer.

"You hear what I said," Rance said. "We need to go."

B.W. looked at Rance, his eyes were glazed. He wiped them with his sleeve. "All hell is goin' to break loose now," B.W. said.

"There's another war coming. May not be with guns but it's coming."

"Can't argue that," Rance said.

A scrubby-looking bartender with slick-down black hair and red garters on his sleeves sat two glasses down in front of them, poured Rance a shot then looked up at B.W., did a double-take and put the cork back in the bottle. "We don't serve Indians," he said.

Rance slid his whiskey glass over in front of B.W., picked up B.W.'s empty glass and sat it in front of him. "I'll have a whiskey," he said. The bartender looked at the glass and then B.W. "You're serving me not him," Rance said. The bartender hesitated, pulled the cork and poured Rance a shot, stuck the cork back in the bottle, picked up the silver dollar and moved away. B.W. didn't say anything, just picked up the glass and downed the whiskey, and Rance did the same.

A big man with an arrogant look wearing a Confederate colonel's uniform stepped away from the bar and walked out into the middle of the floor, his hand on the handle of his saber. He was maybe in his fifties, dark eyes with a neatly trimmed gray beard. He looked around the room, drew his saber and held it up over his head. The piano player quit playing and the saloon became still and quiet.

"You see that flag, boys?" he said, pointing the saber at a Confederate flag on the wall. Everyone yelled a rebel yell. "We have been given another chance. The war's just in a pause now, it's not over. We need to build a new army and march on Washington. Who will join me?" The crowd roared and they sang Dixie again and drank anything that was put in front of them. A voice from the crowd yelled, "We're with you, colonel!" and a roar went up again.

"Already started, major," B.W. said.

"Yeah, all we can do here is get killed," Rance said.

"You wouldn't turn on me, major?" B.W. said.

"What makes you think I would?"

"Have a hard time trusting anyone now."

"War's over," Rance said.

The little thin man was listening. "You was a major?" he asked Rance.

"Was," Rance said. "Forty-first Virginia."

"I was too," the man said. "Buy you a drink. The war may not be over?"

Rance looked at B.W., surprised. B.W. grinned.

The thin man looked at B.W. "He with you, major?"

"He is," Rance said.

The thin man held his glass up again and three fingers, the bartender brought the bottle over and the little man said, "Pour three," and sat his empty glass on the bar beside Rance's and B.W.'s. The bartender hesitated, looking again at B.W., then poured the whiskey.

"Thank you very kindly," B.W. said and gulped the whiskey down.

Rance nudged B.W. "Let's go, we'll get that steak somewhere else," he said and they walked back outside.

Tommy appeared leading the horses. "Wasn't anybody at the livery," he said. "What's goin' on?"

"Lincoln was shot. He's dead," B.W. said. "We'll find another place."

The two rebels doing the shooting outside were passed out in the muddy street.

"Figured you would be happy about this," B.W. said to Rance.

"Nothin' but foolish talk in there," Rance said. "Lincoln was our best hope to put the country back together."

"Yep, gonna be bad for a long time," B.W. said, "especially for the colored. How 'bout we finish off our whiskey to relieve some pain."

"Might be the right time," Rance said.

"Can I have some?" Tommy said.

"Maybe a sip, huh, major?" B.W. said.

"We'll find a quieter place," Rance said and they rode down the street, the horses high-stepping through the mud out of town.

"Lincoln was the president of the Yankees, right?" Tommy asked.

"All of us since they won the war," Rance said.

"Was a special man," B.W. said.

"He was," Rance said. "Got to give him that."

"What you mean,?" Tommy asked.

"He believed all men should be free," B.W. said.

"Even the colored?" Tommy said.

"Yeah, but now he won't get the chance to make it happen." B.W. said.

"That the way you think, major?" Tommy said.

"He was probably the only one that could bring us together. No telling what will happen now," Rance said. "Could be another war. Not much we can do except always do the right thing."

"And right now the right thing to do is get drunk," B.W. said. "Get the whiskey, major."

7

Several hours later, B.W. sat up on a grassy knoll, two empty whiskey bottles lying nearby. Rance was stretched out on the ground a couple feet away and Tommy curled up on his saddle next to him with his saddle blanket over him.

B.W. started to get up, grabbed his head and sat back down. He heard a moan and saw Rance struggling to push himself upright with his good arm.

"Damn," Rance said. "Look what you made me do. I'm in even more pain now. Feels like my head is disconnected from my body."

"I didn't make you do nothing," B.W. said.

"It was your idea," Rance said. "Don't think anything's changed and you got the boy drunk! Still got a bottle I hid in Tommy's saddle bags from you."

"If you didn't want me to know why did you just tell me, dumbass."

"I don't know, whiskey got me all confused," Rance said.

B.W. glanced at the rising sun and the horses and noticed Tommy's wasn't there. "Tommy's horse is gone."

"Think somebody stole him?" Rance asked.

"How the hell would I know?" B.W. said. "Wake Tommy up. I'll saddle the horses if I can get up."

"Get up boy, we lost your horse." Rance said, shaking Tommy. Tommy threw the blanket off and sat up.

"Everything smells like a horse," he said, wrinkling up his nose.

Rance shook his head looking at him.

"Your horse is gone." B.W. said.

"Think someone stole him?" Tommy said to Rance.

"How the hell would I know?" Rance said.

B.W. led the horses over to Rance and Tommy. "Double with me, boy. Leave the saddle here, cover it with some brush, we'll come back and get it when we find your horse."

"What if we don't?" Tommy said.

"Well we'll have to find you another one, won't we?" B.W. said with a frown.

"Boy, you two sure are grouchy this morning," Tommy said. "You do have a bad hangover. Used to see that all the time in the saloon."

B.W. ignored Tommy's comment and looked at Rance. "He doesn't have a homing around here so if he just wandered off maybe he's not too far away."

"Did you tie him, Tommy?" Rance asked.

"I think so," Tommy said.

"But you don't know for sure?"

"No."

"Don't make much sense for someone to steal just one when they could have taken all of them and bushwhacked us, too," B.W. said. "We weren't in any condition to object."

"Let's start making a circle," Rance said. "Keep widenin' it for 'bout a hundred yards out. He's probably just out there grazing but we got to be ready if trouble comes."

Rance drew the Colt from his belt, rolled the cylinder across his left arm to check the rounds and stuck it back in his belt.

They worked the circle from their spot about a half mile out, but no horse.

On the next trip, ranging further out, they spotted smoke and rode inside a tree line toward it and came to an opening with an old barn not more than a rock's throw away.

Three men were sitting by a campfire next to the barn, passing a whiskey bottle around. Three saddled horses were tied to a sapling nearby. None of them were Tommy's horse. The men had rebel soldier caps on and their Remington .44s in a holster on their hips.

B.W. held up a finger to his mouth to indicate silence to Rance and Tommy They dismounted. Rance and B.W. handed the horses' reins to Tommy inside the tree line. B.W. made a staying motion with his hand to Tommy. B.W. stepped out in the opening, pointing the double-barrel toward the men. Rance moved up beside him with his Colt cocked.

"Stay just like you are, boys," B.W. said. "Nobody move, we're lookin' for our horse."

One of the men turned his head toward B.W. and placed his hand on the butt of his revolver.

"You don't want to do that, hombre, I'll blow you apart 'fore you pull it," B.W. said.

The man dropped his hand from the Colt and started to stand.

"Sit down," B.W. said and the man dropped back down to a sitting potion on the tree stump.

He still had that boyish look with bushy blonde hair sticking out from under his rebel cap. The other two didn't move. They looked a little older, similar-looking, same color eyes, about the same height. Maybe brothers. A cooking pot was sitting on the ground by the fire.

"You boys like some grits?" the young one said.

"No thanks," Rance said and noticed a price mark with Catching's Trading Post on the grits box by the pot.

"Can we get up now?" the young one asked.

"Feel better if you just sit right there for now," B.W. said.

"You lawmen?" the young one asked. He may have been the young one but they could tell who the leader was.

"No, just lookin' for a horse," B.W. said. "A roan gelding 'bout fourteen hands, you seen him?"

The brothers were silent and kept glancing at the barn.

"We haven't seen your horse," the young one said. "And I'm gettin' a little nervous lookin' down the barrels of that scatter gun."

"Long as you're looking at it you're okay," B.W. said.

"When were you at Catching's Trading Post?" Rance asked.

Before anyone could answer a scream came from the barn.

The three strangers went for their guns but B.W. cut them down with both barrels of the shotgun as Rance put a bullet in the young one's chest. He fell on his back, drew one leg up and down a couple of times like he was riding a bicycle, exhaled, then didn't move anymore.

B.W. reloaded the shotgun and ran into the barn. A young colored woman wearing a tattered blue cotton dress was hanging from a beam in the barn by her hands, her feet dragging the ground, a dirty neckerchief tied around her neck. She was covered in cuts and bruises, blood trickling down her legs. A bloody gag she spit out was lying on the ground in front of her. A shovel lying nearby had blood on the handle.

There was sheer terror in her eyes as B.W. moved toward her. "It's alright, I'm not going to hurt you." He drew his knife and she screamed again.

"I'm just going to cut the ropes," B.W. said again. He cut her loose from the beam and she fell to the ground. He untied her hands, slung the shotgun strap across his back, picked her up and carried her outside and sat her against a tree.

He kneeled down beside her. "It's okay, we're goin' to take care of you."

Tommy led the horses up to B.W.

"Hand me my canteen, major," B.W. said and Rance retrieved the canteen and handed it to him. He held the canteen while the woman drank and put the cap back on when she had had enough.

"What's your name?" B.W. asked.

"Camille Brookings," she said. "They hung my husband and son. Been raping and torturing me. The boy mostly."

The young one moaned. B.W. turned to look at him, gritted his teeth and handed the woman the canteen, then got up and walked over to the young one. He looked up at B.W., blood running out of his mouth, tried to speak but couldn't. B.W. swung the shotgun from his back, cocked both hammers and pulled the triggers. The young one was nothing more now than a piece of bloody meat.

B.W. walked back to the woman, propped the shotgun against the tree and sat down beside her.

"He won't hurt anyone else," B.W. said and the woman began to cry.

"That wasn't necessary," Rance said. "He was gonna die."

"Was for me," B.W. said.

The woman cupped a hand, poured water in to it and wiped her face and dried it on her dress, then placed the canteen to her lips, gulped water down and handed it back to B.W.

"We found your kin, buried them," B.W. said. "Name's B.W. That's the major and the boy is Tommy."

"Thank you," she said in a whisper. "They did horrible things to me."

"We'll get you to a doctor," B.W. said.

Rance was standing behind B.W. "We'll find a place for you to get well. We got food if you want it."

"Thank you," she said. "Need to rest now."

B.W. got to his feet, opened his saddle bags and took one of the stained gloves out, walked over to the bloody young one and slipped the glove on his hand, a perfect fit.

"Figured it was his," he said.

"Blowing him apart was wrong," Rance said.

"Don't tell me what to think, major. Ma'am, there's a big oak tree up on that little hill with a good shade where you can rest. Why don't I carry you there so you won't have to look at these varmints."

"That would be good, B.W., if it's not too much trouble," she said.

"No trouble at all, ma'am. Tommy, follow me with the horses."

"Go on up with B.W.," Rance said to Tommy. "I'll get the horses."

B.W. picked up Camille and carried her up the hill and sat her down in the shade. He got his bedroll and brought it to her. "Take whatever time you need, ma'am."

"I have been bleedin' and it's gettin' worse, you know what I mean?"

"Yes ma'am. Is there anything we can do?"

"No," she said and tore a strip of cloth from her ragged dress. "Leave me be while I tend to myself."

"Wave if you need us," B.W. said.

She nodded and motion for them to leave.

They walked up to the crest of the hill, sat down and watched the afternoon sun roll shadows across the side of a distant mountain.

"Is it woman trouble?" Tommy said.

"Yes," B.W. said. "They hurt her bad."

"Men did that to my mama," Tommy said and a tear came to his eye.

"Sorry to hear that, boy," B.W. said.

"We going to get her to a doctor?" Tommy asked.

"She's not able to go right now," B.W. said. "Needs to stop the blood first. I'll check on her in a little bit."

"We're not very far from Milberg. They got a doctor there," Rance said.

"We got to make a drag. She can't sit a horse," B.W. said. He stood up and looked down the hill. She wasn't moving. He hurried down the hill, Rance and Tommy following, and saw her lying on her back, her dress soaked in blood. Her eyes were open but there was no movement in them. B.W. kneeled down beside her. "Mrs. Brookings," he said. Nothing. He held his fingers against her neck for a pulse and dropped his head. "She's dead," he said. "She knew she was dying. Tried to make it easy on us."

B.W. took off his hat and sat down beside Camille. Rance and Tommy took off their hats and sat down beside B.W.

B.W. closed her eyes and held her hands. "We took too long to find you. I'm so sorry. Knew you was out here, should have gone lookin' for you sooner."

"You didn't know for sure. Could have been chasing a ghost," Rance said.

"I knew. Just didn't do what my gut told me," B.W. said.

They wrapped her in a bed roll, tied it with a rope. B.W. dug a grave in the shade of the tree. They covered the grave with rocks and B.W. carved 'Camille Brookings died 17 April 1865' on the tree.

"Think we should say something over her?" Rance asked.

"Yeah, say she was unlucky enough to be born the wrong color," B.W. said.

"Won't do her any good but Lincoln changed that," Rance said.

"Maybe. We'll see." B.W. mounted his horse and rode away.

Rance watched B.W. ride down the hill and wondered how much of the killing of those three was for him."

They left the dead rebels where they fell. Threw dirt on the campfire, commandeered a horse for Tommy, let the others loose and headed for Milberg. Rance figured the rebels probably sold Tommy's horse. He knew they made the mistake of their life by not killing them when they stole their horse.

"We should have buried them," Rance said. "It was the right thing to do."

"Well go back and do it," B.W. said, "but I'm not."

"You know damn well I can't with one hand."

"The buzzards will take care of 'em," B.W. said. "Didn't deserve to be buried anyways."

"Everyone deserves a proper burial," Rance said.

"You gonna preach to me now?" B.W. asked.

"No. They needed to pay for what they did, the glove proved that. Just don't want to be like them."

"Don't compare myself with other people, good or bad," B.W. said.

"Maybe you should," Rance said.

They heard a horse nicker and looked toward the sound. There stood the roan, the reins dragging the ground. He threw his head up and trotted over to Tommy.

"Well I'll be damned," Rance said. "He did wander off."

"I'd rather ride him," Tommy said.

"Take him then," B.W. said, "and cut the other one loose."

Tommy saddled the roan, pulled the bridle off the other horse and he took off.

"We goin' back for the other saddle?" Tommy said.

"No," B.W. said. "Let it be. How far to Milberg, major?"

"Bout another two or three hours," Rance said. "Used to be a place called Jack's Eatery and Boarding House in Milberg. If it's still there we can get a good steak and a real bed."

"Been a while since I slept in a bed," B.W. said. "Last time was a disaster. Those two scandals Shanghai'd me."

"Now whose fault was that?" Rance said.

"What happened?" Tommy asked.

"It's a long story, tell you some other time," B.W. said.

"He don't want you to know," Rance said and grinned.

"If it's that big of a deal forget it," Tommy said, spurred his horse into a gallop and rode ahead.

"You know he's goin' to ask you again," Rance said.

"Yeah, thanks to you," B.W. said.

"What you get for bein' in a place you shouldn't be."

"Won't let me forget it, will you?"

"Nope," Rance said and took off after Tommy.

"Horse, we should have went our separate ways," B.W. said and patted him on the neck.

8

As they rode into Milberg, the disappearing sun painted the edge of the western sky a bright orange. Mostly uniformed Union soldiers were going in and out of saloons along the street. Signs were posted on some of the business doors stating they were closed by military authority under martial law for unlawful practice.

They rode past the saloons and saw Jack's Eatery and Boarding House was open.

"There's a livery next door for the horses," Rance said. "Get you a steak and a bed. I'll be back in a while."

"Be waitin' on you," B.W. said.

Rance nodded and rode away.

"Where's he goin?'" Tommy asked.

"To visit his wife and daughter's graves."

By the time Rance got to the graveyard the sun was on its way to another day.

He rode up to the graves, dismounted and looked at the inscriptions on the tombstones in the twilight:

Paige Kendra Allison
May 5 1833 - July 12 1861

Melody Ann Allison
October 11 1854 - July 12 1861.

"Finally made it home, Paige." He touched the tombstones and tears came to his eyes. "Missed you so. Don't really know what to do with myself without you. We lost the war and somebody killed Lincoln, to make it worse. I lost a hand and part of my left arm. The war freed the slaves but it's goin' to take a long time for the south to accept the change. I met up with an Indian-black mix and a boy that's kind of become my family now. We never made any promises to each other but I know I can count on 'em. Want to take care of some unfinished business for the boy in Texas. He's the rightful heir to a railroad company, but his papa disowned him and his mama was murdered. He's a good kid - had some bad breaks, deserves better - a little older than Melody. Feels like the right thing to do. The stars are out, and there's a full moon and a nice breeze. I remember how much you like to sit on the porch, sip your tea and admire a night like this." He dropped his head and stood motionless for a minute or two then wiped his eyes on his sleeve and looked back at the tombstones. "Guess that's all I got for now. I will always love you both. You'll never leave my memory."

He leaned over, kissed the tombstones, rubbed his only hand across the top of the tombstones, pulled himself up on Buck and headed back to town. He turned in the saddle for one last look and rode on.

Back in town, Rance bedded Buck down, picked up his saddle bags, sat them on his shoulder, retrieved the Henry and walked in the eatery. There were five rough wood tables and chairs with red and white checkered curtains on the windows, double swinging doors to the kitchen and a little bar. He sat down at a table by a window and gazed out at the stars, thinking of his wife and daughter.

A pretty red-headed woman with big blue eyes, wearing an apron over a green dress, appeared through the kitchen doors and walked up to the back of his chair. When she saw who it was she sat down hard on a nearby chair gasping for air. "Rance?" she said. "I thought you was dead."

"Hello, Julie. I almost was." He stood up and removed his hat. She threw her arms around him and he hugged her with his good arm. "Sorry to startle you. You all right?"

She kissed him on the cheek. He returned the favor and they stepped back from each other.

"Is it really you?" she asked.

"What's left of me, at least," he said. "You workin' here?"

"Own the place now. Jack was killed at Gettysburg. His wife sold out to me and headed for California."

"Heard from your pa?" he asked.

"Lost my dad at Petersburg and my brother at Manses," she said. "My mama died last spring from a broken heart. Wiped my whole family out."

"Same for me. It's been a terrible time. Ever find you a husband?"

"Never got around to it. All the men went to war. Most didn't come back. Not many of the home folks still here, either. The Yankees declared martial law, closed down some of the businesses for carpetbaggers, even hired them a Yankee marshal. The marshal said an actor named John Wilkes Booth killed Lincoln and they got the biggest manhunt in history goin' on to find him."

"I heard," he said.

"Bet you're hungry," she said. "What can I get you?"

"You got a steak?" Rance said.

"I'll fix you a steak with all the trimmings on the house as a homecoming," she said.

"No need to do that."

"Want to." She walked over to the bar, picked up a glass and a bottle of whiskey and sat them on his table. "Nurse on this while I fix that steak," she said and smiled. "You can take the bottle with you when you go."

"You feed an Indian and a boy tonight?" Rance asked.

"Sure did. They rented a bed and went upstairs. Got you one there if you want it."

"They're friends of mine. We're riding together."

"The beds are ready. Take anyone you want. I'll go fix your steak," she said and walked through the swinging doors to the kitchen, stopped inside the door, leaned against the wall and began to sob.

She placed her apron over her mouth to muffle the sound and continued crying for several minutes. She wiped the tears away with her apron, took a deep breath. "Now what do I do?" she said to herself and picked up a large skillet and sat it on the stove. "Fix the steak and keep my mouth shut," she said to the stove.

Rance was gazing out the window, sipping the whiskey when she brought the steak to him and laid a knife and fork on the table beside the plate, looked at his arm and picked the knife and fork up quicker then she laid them down.

"Sorry," she said. "Should have cut the steak before I brought it out."

"That's okay," he said. "Learning to do a lot of things different now. I can manage."

"Not this time," she said and started cutting the steak. She finished cutting the steak and laid the fork and knife back on the table.

"Thanks," Rance said. "Does a train still come through here?"

"No. Yanks stopped everything from goin' or comin' from Milberg for the time being. Why?"

"Thinkin' 'bout ridin' one to Texas."

"Someone said they're runnin' further down the line, don't know for sure. Why Texas?"

"Need to help the boy get to Texas, settle some things with his old man he can't do by himself."

She nodded. "If you need anything, yell. I have to go clean the kitchen. Enjoy your steak."

Rance nodded and she disappeared through the kitchen doors and stopped to wipe more tears in the kitchen.

"I can't," she said to herself. "I just can't tell him."

Rance finished his steak, stuck the bottle of whiskey in his saddle bags and went upstairs. The door was open. It was a big room with four beds. A quilt was folded at the foot of each bed, a pitcher of water and a wash bowl were on a small table by each bed with a towel and a lit lamp. Tommy was already sound asleep.

A broad-shouldered man with big arms and no neck was sitting on a bed packing something in a sack. He got up, walked by Rance out the open door and closed it without saying a word.

B.W. was sitting on his bed cleaning the twelve-gauge, his tomahawk on the table, his boots by the bed. "Get to see your family's graves?"

"Did. Was hard." Rance sat his weapons and saddle bags on the floor and sat down on the bed. "Julie said she heard the man that killed Lincoln was an actor named John Wilkes Booth."

"I'll be damned! Heard of him, went to a play one time he was in called My American Cousin. Hope they kill that bastard."

"I'm sure they will. Brought you something." Rance handed B.W. the whiskey. "Julie gave it to me. I thought you might need a drink."

"Thanks. That Miss Julie sure is a pretty thing," B.W. said.

"Sure is," Rance said.

"She got a husband?"

"No."

"You know her long?"

"Since we were kids."

"Might be a good idea to get reacquainted," B.W. said.

"Crossed my mind."

There was a knock on the door. B.W. got up and opened it. A pretty young black woman with sparkling brown eyes and skin as smooth as cream was standing there smiling.

"Sorry to bother you," she said. "My name's Fannie. Julie asked me to see if you needed anything 'fore I turned in."

"I'm good. The boy's out cold. How 'bout you, major?" B.W. asked, looking at Rance.

"I'm good too, thank you," Rance said.

"Alright," Fannie said. "Breakfast is at six, have a good night."

"Thank you," B.W. said. Fannie walked out and B.W. closed the door. "Another pretty woman. I'm beginnin' to like it here."

"Nothin' like a woman to make a man feel good 'bout himself," Rance said.

"Yeah, but next time I'm going to sleep with this twelve-gauge, just in case."

"May just need to be more careful where you sleep."

"Yep, there you go again.," B.W. said. "Thought anymore on Texas?"

"Maybe we should go, unless you got other plans. Might be able to do something useful."

"That's important to you, ain't it?" B.W. said, took the cap off the whiskey bottle, took a big swig and put the cap back on.

"What, goin' to Texas?" Rance asked.

"No, doin' something useful," B.W. said.

"Yes it is. You're a lawyer. We can take his old man to court," Rance said.

"Don't know, think I might like killin' him better."

"Now that would solve everything. We wouldn't care after they hang us."

"I hear you, but if the court thing don't work, then I'll kill him."

"I think you missed the part in school 'bout upholding the law."

"Didn't miss it, just don't always agree with it," B.W. said, took the cap off the whiskey bottle and let a big, slow swallow roll down his throat and sighed. "Nectar of the gods."

"Just make sure you don't get scalped." Rance pulled his boots off and laid down on the bed.

B.W. nodded in agreement, put the cap back on the bottle, sat it on the table and laid down on his bed.

"Good to know you're in control instead of the whiskey," Rance said and turned over.

B.W. laid the double-barrel beside him on the bed, wrapped a hand around the whiskey bottle on the table and sat it beside him in the bed, snuggling up to it and closing his eyes.

9

The three of them were the only ones in the eatery enjoying a big plate of biscuits, sorghum and sowbelly, B.W. sipping on his whiskey a little after six in the morning. Julie walked up to their table.

"How's the biscuits?" she asked.

"Ma'am," B.W. said. "These biscuits are so good, I would ask you to marry me if I was a marrying man."

"Ask Fannie then, she made them," Julie said.

"I'll keep that in mind, might do that," he said and smiled.

"Need any more coffee, Rance?" Julie asked.

"Think I'm done, might give B.W. another cup."

"How bout you, Tommy? Want some more milk?" she asked.

"No ma'am," he said.

"I'll stop in before we leave town," Rance said.

"You do that," she said.

The door came open and a tall man with dark eyes and a bushy black mustache walked in. He was wearing a black Stetson, a marshal's badge on his white shirt and a tied-down walnut-handled Colt .44 with the initials W.P. carved into the handle. He sat down at a table by the door.

"What'll you have this morning, marshal?" Julie asked.

"Just coffee," he said, took off his hat, laid it on the table, looked their way and nodded. They nodded back.

They picked up their gear, B.W. paid Julie and they walked out on the board sidewalk.

"That must be the Yankee marshal Julie was tellin' me bout," Rance said.

B.W. nodded.

The streets were empty and they could see people peeking out the windows of some of the stores.

"We do have our pants on, don't we, B.W.?" Rance asked.

"Curious bunch, ain't they?"

The marshal came out of the eatery behind them with his Colt drawn. "Don't make any sudden moves, boys, or it'll be your last. I'm Marshal Willie Preston and you're under arrest."

Three men stepped out of nearby stores with shotguns pointed at them.

"What's going on, marshal?" Rance asked.

"Murder. Got a witness that says you two look like the hombres that murdered a man named Allen Dobbs in Whiskey Gulch. Now, if you'll stand real still, I'll have my boys relieve you of your weapons."

"Who's the witness?" Rance asked.

"Your roommate was in Whiskey Gulch when it happened, come and told me last night," the marshal said. "I locked him up as a witness, figured it was better to do this in the daylight."

"The big fellow with no neck?" Rance asked.

"Name's Lester. He's a miner in the Gulch."

"Wondered why he didn't come back to bed," B.W. said.

Julie heard the commotion and came out on the sidewalk. "What's going on?" she asked.

"We been arrested," Rance said.

"For what?" she asked.

"Murder, but it was self defense."

"You know these men, Miss Julie?" the marshal asked.

"Yes I do."

"I'll have some questions for you later," the marshal said. "Would you look after the boy. Keep him in tow till I figure out what to do with him?"

"Sure," She placed a hand on Tommy's shoulder. "I'll take care of him Rance." Rance and B.W. nodded. "Come with me, Tommy," she said.

"Yes ma'am." They walked back in the eatery.

"You got a name I can pronounce, Indian?" the marshal asked, looking at B.W.

"Black Wind. B.W. for short. Make it easy for you."

"You don't talk like an Indian," the marshal said.

"Educated," Rance said.

"And who might you be, wise-ass ?"

"Rance Allison, sir."

"Where do you boys know Miss Julie from?"

"I grew up here," Rance said. "We owned a farm the Yankees stole."

"You don't say," the marshal said. "May be more to this than murder, then. Take Mr. Allison and this educated Indian to the jail, boys."

Five minutes later, B.W. and Rance were looking out the jail window, another prisoner in the next cell had his hat pulled over his face ,sleeping in the bunk.

"Knew somethin' was wrong with sleepin' in a bed," B.W. said. "Every time I do something bad happens."

"You just sleepin' in the wrong beds," Rance said.

A booming voice from the next cell yelled out. "They gonna hang you!" The man in the cell pulled his hat off his face and sat up.

"Well, it's No-Neck," Rance said. "You gettin' paid to lie?"

"Name's Lester Crayton," he said.

"Well Lester, you know B.W. had to kill him," Rance said.

"It was self-defense," B.W. said. "He was goin' to shoot both of us."

"I know that," Lester said. "But do you think anyone in Whiskey Gulch is goin' to remember it that way? They would kill me if I said that."

"Would think so, you're probably right but we'll make sure we figure out how to kill you before they hang us." B.W. said.

They heard the door rattle to the cell room and a big ornery-looking brute, almost as big as B.W., with thick blonde hair walked in with an ivory-handled Colt on his belt.

"Name's Charlie Caldwell, deputy marshal. If you're expectin' lunch, forget it," he said. "We feed you two meals a day - breakfast and dinner from Jake's Eatery. There's a water bucket by your cell with a dipper. If you have to go to the outhouse, run the dipper on the bars. Has to be one at a time."

"All the comforts of home," Rance said.

"You won't be so cute when your feet are kickin' air."

"What about me?" No-Neck said. "I'm not a prisoner, I'm a witness."

"You're in the jail. Same applies to you." He walked out and they heard the lock turn on the cell door.

"Did you see that gun he was wearing?" B.W. asked.

"A Colt," Rance said.

"Was one of those new double-action French Colts. You don't have to cock it. That's what you need."

"Don't think he's goin' to sell or give it to me."

"No, but we might relieve him of it," B.W. said.

"Well when you figure out how, let me know."

"I'll do that," B.W. said as he stared out the window at the hanging gallows at the end of the street.

In the eatery, Julie sat Tommy down and brought him a glass of milk and sat down with him.

"How old are you?" she asked.

"Twelve."

"Okay, young man. I know you've been ridin' with Rance and B.W. Tell me the truth. What's going on? Did they murder anyone?"

"Not exactly. B.W. and the major stopped at Whiskey Gulch to get a bath and a whore and everything went wrong."

"To get a what?" she said, her big blue eyes batting like a flying bird.

"A bath and a whore."

Julie shook her head. "You sure you're twelve years old?"

"Yes ma'am. I followed B.W. to the saloon and was watchin' through the window. Some men was holdin' the major, makin' him drink whiskey. One of them pulled a gun and B.W. killed him with his tomahawk and I ran back to the stable and saddled their hoses. B.W. knew I didn't have any folks and asked me to come with them. I have to get them out of jail. There's some other things might come up we ran into after that."

"Like what?"

"Don't want to talk about it right now," Tommy said. "Will you help me get them out of jail?"

"I got to live here," she said. "Don't have any other place to go."

"You could go with us," Tommy said.

"Don't think that's a good idea," she said. "But maybe If I give you my papa's gun we might can surprise them. The deputy will let me in when I take them their supper. They know I have to keep you in tow so you can come in with me. Usually there's only one deputy. Hold the gun on the deputy, I'll tell them you stole it. Tell him to open their cell and you'll be long gone before anyone else knows what happened, and then I won't have to leave town."

"I knew you was a smart lady," Tommy said.

"I hope so, for everybody's sake," she said. "I feed the prisoners about five in the evening. I'll get the gun."

B.W. and Rance were stretched out on their bunks when they heard the lock turn. The marshal walked in the cell, put his hand on the butt of his Colt and looked at them, and they sat up on the bunks.

"Had a farmer bring in three bodies," he said. "Looks like they was blown away and pecked on by some buzzards. Too much of a mess to tell who they were or what they looked like. Sent 'em to the undertaker. That your doin' too?"

B.W. and Rance looked at each other then back to the marshal. "Got nothing to say," B.W. said.

"Well, don't really matter," the marshal said. "Can't hang you twice. Thought you might want to clear your consciences."

"Hang 'em for that and let me outta here," No-Neck said from the next cell.

"This one's easier with you as a witness," the marshal said and walked out the door and the lock snapped.

"Told you we should have buried them," Rance said. B.W. shook his head and laid down.

At five o'clock, Julie and Tommy were ready to put their plan into action. Julie placed the food in a basket and Tommy stuck the Navy Colt in the back of his pants and covered it with his shirt. They headed for the jail.

Julie knocked on the jail door.

"Who is it?" the deputy asked.

"Brought the prisoner's supper."

The door opened. Julie and Tommy walked in and Charlie closed the door.

"Sit the basket on the desk," Charlie said. "I'll give it to them."

Julie sat the basket on the desk and Tommy drew the Colt. "Don't move," he said.

The deputy looked at Tommy and laughed. "What do you think you're doin' boy? Give me that gun 'fore I take it away from you and spank your butt."

The deputy eased his hand toward the Colt on his belt.

"Don't do it, mister. I may not be very big but I don't have to be with this. I'll shoot you." He cocked the Colt.

"Miss Julie, get the keys and open their cell," Tommy said.

Julie picked up the keys from the desk, unlocked the cell room door and walked up to their cell.

"What you doin' here?" Rance asked.

"I was bringin' your supper and Tommy pulled a gun." She winked at Rance and handed him the cell keys.

"Let me out, too," No-Neck said.

"You're on your own," Rance said.

Rance unlocked their cell and they moved out to the front office. The deputy was standing behind his desk, hands up, Tommy holding the gun on him. Rance laid the keys on the desk, lifted the deputy's gun from his holster, eyed the gun and smiled.

"Take off the belt and hand it to me," Rance said.

The deputy took off the belt and handed it to him. He laid the Colt on the desk, swung the belt around his waist with his right hand, held it next to his side with his left arm, ran the belt through the buckle with his right and tightened it, picked up the Colt and pointed it at the deputy.

B.W. picked up the keys, shoved the deputy through the cell room door, locked him in the cell, closed the door, locked it and pitched the keys on the desk.

"You're somethin' else, boy," B.W. said and patted Tommy on the head.

"We better get out of here fast," Tommy said and stuck the gun in his pants.

"What do we do 'bout you, Julie?" Rance asked.

"Nothin,'" Julie said. "I'll be fine. Me and Tommy had a plan, he can tell you 'bout it later. If you're ever back this way, I'll be here." She planted a big kiss on Rance's lips.

"Why don't you go to Texas with us?" Rance asked.

Julie shook her head no. "Not now. I have something to tell you but this isn't the time."

"Tell me," Rance said.

"Later," she said. "I'll find you. Go now."

"I got the horses behind the jail," Tommy said.

B.W. collected his guns and tomahawk, stopped at the door and looked at Julie. "Thanks, Miss Julie."

She smiled and nodded.

"Thanks from me too," Tommy said.

Rance hugged her neck with his good arm.

"You'll get a letter later to tell you where I am if you need me. May be a different name but it will be me."

"Go," she said and they darted out the door and ran to their horses. They mounted and spurred their horses out into the street. Two bystanders across the street were staring at them as they rode out of town.

"That's the prisoners," one of them said. "I'll go get the marshal, you check on the deputy."

10

A man wearing a straw hat, overalls and clod hoppers, with a tobacco sack string hanging out of his chest pocket ran into the saloon out of breath and stopped at a table where Marshal Preston was playing poker.

"Marshal," he said, trying to catch his breath, "got something to tell you."

"Can't you see I'm busy, Floyd?"

"It's important, the prisoners escaped. I saw them high-tailing it out of town."

"Holy shit!" The marshal threw the cards on the table, stood up and picked up his money. "I had a winning hand."

He charged out of the saloon and hurried to the jail. Julie was coming out the jail door.

"What you doin' in there?" he asked Julie.

"Brought the prisoner's supper."

"Was that before or after they escaped?"

"Before. Charlie told me to go home."

"Come back in with me," he said and they walked back in the jail. Charlie and another man named Luke Sewell, was in the jail with Charlie. He had a floppy felt hat on his head a fat face and a bulging waist line. Much like Charlie.

"What happened, Charlie?" the marshal asked.

"That boy pulled a gun and they locked me in a cell and escaped. Luke here let me out."

"You let a kid bully you in to a jail break?"

"He ain't no ordinary kid. He would have shot me! Said to not let the other fellow out."

"You see which way they went?" the marshal asked Luke.

"Saw 'em heading south 'fore I came to the jail," Luke said.

"We better get after them, marshal," Charlie said.

"We're not goin' to catch them in the dark with a head start on us. Miss Julie, you have anything to do with this?"

"You told me to keep an eye on the boy. He stole my gun and forced Charlie to let them out."

"That's what happened," Charlie said.

"Looks like you didn't keep a very good eye on him," the marshal said.

"Afraid not," she said.

"Allison have any kin here?"

"Not anymore. Yankees killed them all."

"I heard one of them say somethin' 'bout Texas," Charlie said. "Couldn't make out much from where I was but he I know he said Texas."

"That where they goin', Julie?" the marshal asked.

"I don't know."

"You're not going to tell me, are you?"

"Told you, I don't know. The boy had a gun."

"This doesn't sound like something a kid cooked up by himself."

"I wouldn't know. Can I go now?"

"For now," he said. "I may want to talk to you again."

She nodded and walked out the door.

"Charlie, round up the other deputies and get that tracker," the marshal said. "I intend to find them no matter how long it takes. Never had a prisoner get away and I'm not going to this time, especially one set free by a kid. Anyone don't think they're up to it can find another job. Get going."

"Yes sir." Charlie opened the door and was gone.

The marshal unlocked the cell room door and walked up to No-Neck's cell.

"You don't need me anymore, let me out of here," No-Neck said.

"Was there any conversation between Allison and Miss Julie?" Preston asked.

"He just asked what she was doing here, that was it. Allison looked surprised to see her."

"I'm goin' to let you out but you better be where I can find you when I need you," the marshal said and unlocked the cell.

"Yes sir, I will," No-Neck said and ran out the door.

Preston walked back to the front office, unlocked the gun cabinet and took the rifles and shotguns out and leaned them on the desk. He loaded a double-barrel, spun the cylinder on his .44 to see if it was fully loaded, lifted his right pants leg up and checked the Arkansas tooth pick inside his right boot and put his pants leg back down over the boot.

The door opened and a Union Army colonel walked in with an arrogant strut. His blonde hair to his shoulders, his deep-set blue eyes gave the illusion he was always staring.

"Hear your prisoners got away," he said.

"Not for long. I'm goin' to get 'em back."

"Don't think that's a good idea. Need you here. Put out a telegram to all law enforcement, let someone else catch them."

"Colonel Hatch, I ain't ever had a prisoner escape and it ain't goin' to be now. When folks find out it was engineered by a kid I'll be the laughing stock of the country. If I don't bring 'em back, I could never marshal anywhere again."

"Not what I've been ordered to do," Colonel Hatch said. "The government wants a civilian face on things here, keep the troops in the background. You keep playing the role of marshal. Of course, everyone knows who's running things."

"You don't give theses people much credit for any smarts, Colonel. They're not going to put up with you much longer." Preston reached up to the marshal's badge on his shirt and pulled it off and handed it to the colonel. "Get you another flunky. I'm going to defend my reputation. I'll take this shotgun as a bonus. Luke, tell Charlie to forget the posse, they're on their own."

"You can't just walk out," Colonel Hatch said.

"Watch me," Preston said.

"I'll have you arrested."

"I wouldn't do that, colonel, you don't want to get acquainted with this shotgun."

"Are you threatening me?"

"Not unless you try to stop me." Preston walked out, leaving Colonel Hatch standing in the jail alone and walked up to the eatery.

There was a CLOSED sign on the door. He banged on the door until Julie opened it.

"What you want?" she asked, wrapping her housecoat tighter around her waist. "You got me out of bed."

Preston stepped in the doorway.

"I just quit, gave Hatch my badge. But I'm still going after Allison and the Indian. I need to know where they're headed."

"I told you, I don't know."

"You're lyin' to me," Preston said.

"I don't have to answer you. You're not the marshal anymore."

The kitchen door swung open and Fannie came in carrying a small boy with wavy black hair and black eyes. "Everything okay, Julie?" she asked.

"Boy's a dead ringer for Allison, with those eyes," Preston said. "That his kid?"

A tear rolled down Julie's cheek.

A slight grin crossed his face and he looked at the boy. "He don't know 'bout the kid, does he?"

"Fannie, take Mitchell back to bed," Julie said.

Fannie nodded and disappeared through the kitchen door.

"Leave me alone. I don't know where Rance is and I wouldn't tell you if I did."

"Charlie said he heard him say they were going to Texas. I'll find him and I'll make sure I tell him he's got a kid he don't know about."

"Please, don't."

"Then it is his kid?"

"Go away!" She started pushing him out of the door.

"I'll find him," he said and stepped back out on the street.

Julie locked the door and sat down on a chair and began to sob.

11

It was long into the night when Rance pulled up Buck and motioned for B.W. and Tommy to stop and they rode up beside him.

"Think they'll come after us?" Tommy asked.

"You can count on it," Rance said. "The man's a professional or they wouldn't have hired him. If he lets us get away his marshaling days are over. He's going to keep comin' for us."

"You think he would chase us all the way to Texas?"

"Depends on how bad he wants us," B.W. said. "He's a federal marshal, he has the authority to follow us anywhere. Guess we'll have to kill him if he does."

"Hope not," Rance said. "Think we're a ways ahead. Might stop for a while, rest the horses."

"I got some biscuits Miss Julie gave me," Tommy said.

"I do love those biscuits," B.W. said. "I'm goin' to have to get better acquainted with Miss Fannie."

They dismounted, Tommy got the biscuits and B.W. got a whiskey bottle out of Tommy's saddle bags.

"Don't say nothin,' Major. I need a drink."

B.W. sat down, took a bite of biscuit and a swig of whiskey.

Rance and Tommy looked at each other and shook their shoulders like they had a chill.

"How can you do that?" Rance asked B.W.

"Do what?"

"Eat biscuits and drink whiskey."

"Won't that make you sick?" Tommy asked.

"Naw, it's good together," B.W. said. "Want some?"

Tommy and Rance shook their head no.

"Remember your promise," Rance said.

"I know," B.W. said. "Tommy, put the bottle back in my saddle bags for me."

"Gladly," Tommy said. "You're making me sick watchin' you."

"We can bed down here till daylight," Rance said. "B.W., you take the first watch, I'll relieve you. Tommy, loosen the girth on the horses, leave the saddles on. It will be your job to tighten them if we have to leave in a hurry. And Put Julie's Colt in your saddle bags before you blow your pecker off."

"He likes givin' orders, don't he, B.W.?" Tommy said.

"Yes he does. Makes him feel useful."

"Quit talking and bed down," Rance said. "We're goin' to be movin' into your part of the country soon, B.W."

"He's giving orders again," Tommy said.

"Comes natural," B.W. said. "Don't want to stay round here very long, could wind up getting scalped by my own people."

"Be moving into Arkansas in a day or two," Rance said. "They won't like you either."

"Kinda that way for the rest of the journey," B.W. said. "But I think they'll think I'm a confederate from my tribe's actions. If you don't tell them different."

"We're not goin' to say anything," Rance said. "Let's get some rest."

They were up at the crack of dawn, riding through a field with thick morning dew, the horse's legs wet past their hocks. They spotted a log cabin in an open field with a corral and small barn nearby and rode in slow.

"Might see if we can get some food and water here," Rance said.

"Don't see any animals in the corral and no smoke from the chimney," B.W. said.

They stopped their horses at a water trough by the corral to let them drink. Th windows were boarded up. Two arrows were stuck in the side of a well curb. B.W. rode by the well, reached down and broke an arrow off the well and looked at it.

"Creek, stay on your horses," he said. "I'll see if I can raise anyone. He dismounted, took the shotgun off the saddle and walked up on the porch and knocked on the door. "Hello in there," he said. No answer. "Anybody in there?" He pounded on the door again. The door exploded, fragments flying everywhere, just missing his arm. He hit the ground and slid up against the cabin.

"Get," Rance yelled at Tommy and they rode their horses to the side of the cabin and dismounted.

Tommy retrieved the Colt from his saddle bags and moved up beside Rance.

"Stay down," Rance said. "B.W., you alright?"

"Yeah," B.W. said. "Hey, in the cabin, I'm an Indian but we're not here to hurt you."

"Don't come no closer," they heard a female voice say from inside. "I'll shoot you."

"Ma'am, we mean you no harm. I'm not a hostile," B.W. said.

"Go away," she said.

"I'm goin' to lay my guns down and walk out where you can see me. I'm an Indian but not one of them. Don't shoot, we mean you no harm."

B.W. laid the shotgun and Colt on the ground, stuck his tomahawk in the back of his belt and walked out in front of the door with his hands up.

Tommy whispered to Rance, "He gone loco?"

"That's far enough. I can see you," she said. "Now get 'fore I turn this shotgun on you."

B.W. glanced to the side of the cabin and Rance was making a circle motioning to indicate he was going to the back of the cabin.

"We just wanted to make sure everyone was okay 'fore we moved on," B.W. said.

"We're fine. Now leave us alone."

B.W. flashed two, then three fingers to indicate to Rance there was more than one in the cabin. Rance nodded and moved to the back of the cabin and snuck up to a boarded-up window and peeked through a gap at the bottom and saw a handsome woman with long blonde hair pinned back wearing a broad rim black felt hat, black pants and a lacy white shirt. She was holding a double-barrel shotgun with a girl about Tommy's age clinging to her.

The woman glanced toward the window, saw Rance and turned the shotgun to the window. Rance hit the ground. She pulled both triggers, blowing the window out.

B.W. charged the door and knocked what was left of it down with his foot. The woman was trying to reload the shotgun. He swung his shotgun strap over his shoulder, grabbed her shotgun, twisted it from her, dropped it on the floor and put her in a bear hug. "I got her!" B.W. yelled.

"Run," the woman said and the girl ran toward the door. Rance and Tommy were coming in the door.

Rance picked her off her feet with his good arm and carried her back in the cabin and sat her down.

"Calm down, please," Rance said.

The woman was still struggling with B.W. "Okay, I'm going to turn you loose," B.W. said and released her. "It's okay."

"Please don't hurt my baby." She began to cry.

"We're not, I promise," Rance said.

She drew the girl close to her and continued to sob.

"Ma'am, it's okay. My name's Rance, this is B.W. and the boy is Tommy. How come you're out here alone?"

"My husband went to Bridgeport for supplies and was supposed to be back before dark yesterday but he didn't come back. We hid in the floor cellar and they stole our livestock and everything else they could carry."

"Did you shoot at them?" B.W. asked.

"No, we went to the cellar as soon as we saw them."

"That saved your life."

"What kind of Indian are you?," she asked B.W.

"Cherokee, ma'am. They was Creek."

"How far is Bridgeport?" Rance asked.

"Bout ten miles," she said.

"We'll escort you and your daughter to town."

"I think I better stay here, wait for my husband."

"Ma'am, they may have bushwhacked your husband and if so, he ain't coming back," Rance said. "You have to leave. What's your name?"

"April Brown," she said. "And this is my daughter May."

Rance smiled. "Clever names," he said. "We better get a move on 'fore those Creeks come back."

"I'll get some riding pants for May and a change of clothes to take with us," she said and went to get them. Rance ,B.W. and Tommy walked outside to wait and Tommy put the Colt back in his saddle bags.

"How did you know you weren't going to get shot when you went through that door?" Rance asked.

"I didn't," B.W. said. "Figured one shooter with a double-barrel and they had to reload."

"I knew that but you didn't."

"Listenin' to my gut."

"Your gut's goin' to get you killed one of these days."

B.W. shrugged. "You know this is going to slow us down and give the marshal time to catch up."

"We can't leave them," Rance said.

"Nope, guess we can't," B.W. said. "Lots of open hoof prints and some wagon tracks, they were probably hungry."

"Hope we don't run into any," Rance said.

"This is Creek and Cherokee country," B.W. said. "Never know what they're going to do. Her husband may be tied to a tree somewhere with his eyes cut out to keep him from seein' in the after world."

"You're full of good news," Rance said.

"Way it is."

April came out of the cabin carrying her shotgun and a small sack, May right behind her wearing pants. Rance forced the shotgun in the saddle boot with the Henry, tied April's sack to the saddle horn and she climbed on Buck with Rance.

"Tommy, let May ride with you," B.W. said and helped her on the horse.

"Your name Tommy?" May asked.

"Yes," Tommy said.

"My name's May."

"I heard."

"I can read."

"Well I can't," Tommy said.

"How come?"

"Cause I don't know how. I'm not a girl."

"What's being a girl got to do with it?"

"Don't know. Don't want to talk."

"One of them men your papa?" she asked.

"No. I'm on my own."

"You're too little to be on your own."

"Well, I am anyways, now hang on." He kicked his horse and they galloped away.

B.W. rode out ahead and disappeared over a rise not too far away.

"Where's he goin?'" April asked.

THE LAST GOOD DAY

"To make sure we don't get any surprises and to look for your husband along the way," Rance said. "We have to keep moving to catch up."

About a mile down the trail, B.W. was waiting for them.

"Haven't seen any hostiles or white men," he said. "Let's keep movin' till we get to Bridgeport. They might be comin' back."

They kept the Henrys lying across their saddles, cocked and ready as they rode along. B.W.'s shotgun still strapped to the side of his saddle.

They were tired and hungry when they got to Bridgeport, B.W. and Rance watching out for Paxton.

Bridgeport, Carolina was like a hundred other little towns. Saloons, livery, jail and a mercantile store, plus various kinds of services. The stores were busy and the saloons were full with drunks coming and going.

Rance rode up to a cowboy on the street. "You got a place to eat around here beside the saloons?"

"Ma's Café," the man said. "Down the street on the right."

"Thanks," Rance said and they rode on down the street.

A two-horse team pulling a wagon stopped at the Wilson Goods Store and a rugged-looking bearded man with a big brim hat wearing overalls jumped down and went into the store.

"That looks like our team," April said.

"Where?" Rance asked.

"The one with the blazed face horse at the store, but that wasn't my husband that went inside."

"B.W.," Rance called. "April thinks that's her team at the Wilson store."

B.W. wheeled his horse around. "Let's have a look," he said and they rode up to the store hitching post, dismounted and tied the horses beside the wagon.

"Tommy, you and May stay with the horses for now," B.W. said.

"I want to know what's going on, too," Tommy said.

"Need you to keep an eye on May and the horses," B.W. said. "I'll let you know when you can come in."

"Don't leave us out here too long," Tommy said.

B.W. nodded and they walked in the store. The man that got down from the wagon was talking to the store clerk.

"Need what's on this list, Alfie," he said and handed the clerk a piece of paper.

The clerk nodded. "Take a little bit, Norman."

Norman nodded.

Rance walked up beside the man. "That your rig out front?" he asked.

"Yeah."

"Where'd you get it?"

"None of your damn business," Norman said.

"Might be," Rance said. "This lady thinks it's hers."

"Well it ain't."

"Mister, we're tryin' to make this easy," B.W. said. "But if you don't tell us where you got that team we may have to do it the hard way."

"Like what?"

B.W. grabbed Norman by his overalls shoulder strap, drew the Colt, cocked the hammer and placed it against the man's head. "Now, where did you get the damn team?"

"I won it in a poker game, fair and square."

"When?" Rance asked.

"Last night from a fellow named Cletus Brown."

"That your husband, ma'am?" B.W. asked.

"Yes," she said.

B.W. let go of Norman, let the hammer down slowly on the Colt and stuck it back in his holster.

"You know where Cletus is, mister?" Rance asked.

"No, we was at the Crow's Nest last night. May still be there was cuddling with one of the whores."

"If that's what happened we won't bother you again," B.W. said. "If it's not...we will."

"Like I said, won it fair and square. He put it up for his hand. I had three aces, he had three jacks, everybody at the table saw it."

"I don't believe that," April said. "He would never do that."

"We'll find out," Rance said.

"You got no right poking a gun at me," Norman said, shaking his fist at B.W.

"Maybe," B.W. said. "If you want to keep that hand don't shake your fist at me again."

Norman glanced at his hand and dropped it by his side.

B.W. nodded approval and they walked out.

"What's goin' on?" Tommy asked.

"We're not sure yet," B.W. said.

"Ain't doin' no more babysittin'," Tommy said.

"I ain't no baby," May said. "I'm 'bout old as you are."

"You're a girl," Tommy said.

"Bet I can whip you," May said, staring at Tommy.

"I don't fight girls."

"May, mind your manners," April said. "Hush."

Tommy looked at May and smiled.

"Wonder where my husband is?" April said.

"He's most likely still in town, ma'am," Rance said. "If what the man said is true unless he walked out of town. What's he look like?"

"Bout the same age and size as you," she said, "a short black beard and blue eyes. Can't believe he would gamble our team away."

"If he was drunk, he might do anything. Right, B.W.?"

B.W. gave Rance a sideways look. "Right."

"Ma'am, you and the kids go to the cafe and get something to eat," Rance said. "We'll see if we can find your husband."

"Suits me," Tommy said. "I'm hungry as a bear."

"Take the horses with you, Tommy, we'll walk," B.W. said.

Rance and B.W. walked in the Crow's Nest up to the bar. A large picture of a naked lady with a sheet covering her butt was hanging on the wall behind the bar. The bar was crowded with men still wearing their Union and Confederate uniforms. A piano player was playing what sounded like an Irish tune and a little whore was trying to give her best impression of an Irish jig.

The man behind the bar was average size, thinning gray hair, a droopy gray mustache and a gold watch chain looped in his vest pocket. A grin came on B.W.'s face as he stared at the bartender. For some reason it occurred to him that although the bartenders looked somewhat different from town to town, they were all the same with sleeve garters, aprons and a short fuse.

"Two whiskeys," B.W. said.

"What you grinnin' at?" the bartender asked. "Federals don't like us servin' Indians."

B.W. laid his Colt on the bar. "Well, make an exception 'fore I lose my sense of humor."

The man looked at the Colt, wiped his brow and came back with a bottle and glasses and poured the drinks.

"Fifty cents a drink," he said and held out his hand. B.W. reached in his pocket, took out a silver dollar.

"You know a man named Cletus Brown?" Rance asked.

"Tell you for another one of those silver dollars."

B.W. pitched a dollar on the bar and the little man scooped it up. "Seen him here enough to know who he is. That's 'bout all."

"Was he playin' poker last night?"

"Yeah, was drunk, lost his wagon and horses to Norman Stiles."

"You know where he is?" B.W. asked.

"Gave a whore his watch and went upstairs to sleep it off last night. Ain't come down as far as I know."

"What room?" Rance said.

"Room five. Why all the questions? You the law or something?"

"Mostly something," Rance said.

B.W. picked up his whiskey glass, downed the whiskey, and Rance did the same. They went upstairs to room number five and walked up to the door.

"Don't think he's goin' to be in any mood to greet a couple of strangers," B.W. whispered.

Rance nodded and they drew their pistols. B.W. turned the door handle easy-like. It wasn't locked. When he opened the door they saw a man that fit the description April gave them in his long-johns, his boots on, sprawled across the bed with a young naked woman next to him laying on her stomach, both sound asleep. Their clothes lay at the foot of the bed, a carbine propped up in a corner next to the door.

B.W. shook the bed. "You Cletus Brown?" he said and the man turned his head toward them, opened one eye.

"Go away," he said and dropped his head back on the bed and closed his eyes.

B.W. and Rance looked at each other and Rance made a lifting motion and B.W. nodded. They put their guns away, grabbed the mattress, picked it up and flipped it over. The woman crawled out from under the bed, wrapped a sheet around her and ran out of the room without saying a word. Cletus crawled out on his hands and knees, picked up his pants, pulled himself up on a chair and sat down. He was trying to put his pants on over his boots.

"That would be easier if you take the boots off first," Rance said.

"Who the hell are you?"

"We found your wife and daughter after an Indian attack. They managed to survive by hiding in the cellar. The Indians took your stock and most everything else."

"Oh my god," he said, dropped his pants on the floor, put his head in his hands. "You bring 'em here?"

"Yes. Get dressed, they're waitin' for you at Ma's Café," Rance said.

"Not anymore," a woman's voice said from behind them. They turned to the door and April was standing there, holding the carbine. "It's true. You did do it, and left me and May to die."

"I was drunk. I don't remember what I did."

"So long, Cletus." She aimed the carbine at him but B.W. pushed the barrel up just as she pulled the triggers and she shot a hole in the ceiling, debris falling on the bed. Cletus scampered under the bed, his boots sticking out.

"Give me the gun," Rance said. "He ain't worth killin' over."

She started to cry and he took the carbine from her.

"Cletus Brown, you can go to hell. I'm goin' back to Virginia," she said, looking at Cletus' boots. She wiped her eyes and hurried out the door.

"You can come out now," B.W. said. "The big bad wolf is gone, you sorry sonofabitch."

The bed came flying up in the air, Cletus stood up wild-eyed, slobbering like a mad dog and made a lunge for the carbine. B.W. kicked him away and slammed the barrel of his Colt hard against his head.

Blood flew out of a big gash on his head and he staggered backwards and fell on the overturned bed.

B.W. picked up the carbine, opened the window and threw it outside.

Cletus moaned and sat up, wiping the blood from his head with a sheet.

"Stay away from April and May or we'll kill you. You understand?" B.W. said.

"Who are you?" Cletus asked, dabbing at the blood on his forehead with the sheet.

"Don't matter. Do what we said." Rance said and they walked out.

They bought her and May a stage ticket bound for Roanoke, Virginia and gave her twenty dollars of Jake's money.

May kept goading Tommy right up to the time the stage pulled out, telling him she could beat him up.

Tommy had pretty well ignored her, and nothing infuriates a female more then to be ignored at any age.

After April and May left, Rance, B.W. and Tommy ate at Ma's, watered and fed their horses, gave the livery owner an extra buck and rode out of town to get more ground between them and the marshal.

12

They got up at daybreak and saddled their horses. Tommy fixed some flapjacks.

"Hope that lady and her daughter make it back to Virginia okay," B.W. said.

"That crazy kid of hers needs a spanking," Tommy said. "Wantin' to fight me."

"You did the right thing, Tommy, we don't hit girls," Rance said.

"Well that didn't matter to the men my mama saw. A lot of them would beat the hell out of her for no good reason."

"I'll do the cussin', Tommy," B.W. said.

"Those kind are not men, Tommy , they're scum," Rance said.

"Do you know who shot your mama?" B.W. asked.

"I think so," Tommy said. "I was washing glasses at the bar when I heard a shot and my mama screaming. I ran up the stairs and a man ran out of our room, shovin' me and runnin' down the stairs. I noticed he had pearl-handled pistols and fancy boots as he ran past me. I followed him out of the saloon. He jumped on a bay horse and rode out of town as fast as he could go. When I got back to our room my mama was dead. The sheriff never even went after him."

"What kind of fancy boots?" Rance asked.

"They were red and black with a longhorn cow on them. I can still see them."

"Sounds like Texas longhorns," Rance said.

"Sure does," B.W. said. "They have cows in Texas, Tommy, that have longer horns than anywhere else. He may have been from Texas."

"Nobody had ever seen him before," Tommy said.

"That may be why," B.W. said.

"You thinkin' what I'm thinkin' B.W.?" Rance said.

"Yeah, could be. Your mama say anything 'bout trouble 'fore she was killed?" he asked Tommy

"No, nothing."

"Anything else?" Rance said.

"Just that we was goin' back to Texas to get what was ours and my papa might not like it."

"Guess we'll have to be on the lookout for those boots when we get to Texas," B.W. said. "May be a thousand pair or one, if they was custom made."

"If we can get there in one piece," Rance said.

"How would the marshal know where we're going if Miss Julie don't tell him?" Tommy said.

"She won't, but men like that are trained to know," Rance said. "Pretty sure he's figured it out by bnow. If we can find a cattle train going to Texas, we could get there a lot quicker. Maybe on one of your daddy's trains."

As they rode on, dark clouds began to gather in the distance and lightning flashed across the sky.

"Look at that," B.W. said. "Bad stuff comin,' we got to get out of the open."

"If we got time to get to that over yonder we can get some cover," Rance said, gesturing toward the nearest mountain. "Don't see nothin' else but prairie grass between us and that mountain."

"Think we can make it 'fore it gets here?" Tommy said.

"Have to," Rance said and they took off.

They could see a hard rain in the distance and the lightning darting back and forth across the sky.

Suddenly, the lightning stopped and it became still and quiet—no birds in the sky and no sounds of animals.

They rode to the foot of the mountain and saw what looked like the entrance to an old mine shaft a little ways up and rode to it.

"Looks like this one petered out some time ago," Rance said. "If that storm is as big as it looks from here, this is where we need to hunker down."

"I ain't goin' in there," Tommy said. "Why don't we head a different direction and outrun it?"

"Too wide," Rance said.

"Don't like it either," B.W. said, "but it may be like the major said: We ain't got a choice."

"Don't have to go in too far, just enough to protect us from the wind and wait till it passes. Watch for snakes," Rance said.

"I hate snakes," Tommy said.

"I'll go in first." Rance led Buck through the weeds and into the mine shaft. Tommy and B.W. followed.

"Boy, does this place stink," Tommy said.

"Animals usin' it too," B.W. said.

"They can have it."

"Not just yet," Rance said.

The roar of the storm picked up again and they held on to their horses. The rain started and in seconds it looked like a dark gray curtain had been pulled down over the entrance to the mine. The rain came in waves as the wind whistled across the mountain, blowing away everything in its path. The horses pranced, pawing at the ground as they held on. They knew if one got away he was a dead horse. B.W. grabbed the reins of Tommy's horse and helped him hang on. In less than five minutes the storm had moved across the mountain and was sweeping the prairie clean.

They led their horses out of the mine shaft and breathed a sigh of relief. An old overturned rusted ore car was laying on a rail track with Westway Copper Mine on the side of it.

"What's that say on that car?" Tommy asked.

"Westway Copper Mine," Rance said.

"Would you and B.W. learn me to read?"

"Sure," Rance said.

"When?"

"Don't know, exactly," Rance said.

"Soon," B.W. said.

"I need to be able to read things."

They followed the mine rails through weeds and brush and saw a railroad track and an old busted-down loading dock with a spur that ran to railroad tracks. The tracks ran north and south as far as they could see.

"Tracks look clean and shiny, may be a train is using them now," Rance said. "Let's follow the tracks. One might come along headed south."

"Why can't we just wait for it here?" Tommy said.

"We would be givin' that marshal catchin'-up time," B.W. said.

"Need to find a place the train would stop," Rance said.

As they rode along beside the tracks, they could see the storm moving further away and the mist in the air evaporating fast. They followed the tracks for three days, and when the sun was hanging on the late afternoon side of the sky that third day, they heard a train whistle.

"Hear that?" Tommy said.

"That could be the one we're lookin' for. It's whistling for a stop," Rance said. "We got to get to wherever it stops before they do. Let's ride."

They spurred their horses into a gallop, looking for a place the train would stop. As they rounded a bend they saw a railroad water tower. They rode up to a hitching post behind the tower, dropped down from their horses and tied them snugly to a hitching post and stepped up on the platform.

"Hope we don't scare them off," Rance said.

A big black locomotive painted with Number Seventy-Six on the cattle guard and Union Pacific on the side came around the bend, huffing and puffing, blowing smoke high into the air, pulling a bunch of cattle cars. By the time it reached the platform you could walk faster than it was traveling, steel-on-steel grinding to a halt. Steam shot out of the engine and the whistle blew. Buck, B.W.'s horse and Tommy's roan danced a little, but they were use to the loud noises from the war.

A man stepped down from the locomotive to the platform and stretched his arms over his head and looked around. He was tall and gaunt-looking, maybe in his fifties, wearing a Union Pacific railroad cap and red suspenders. Another man, shorter and heavier than the first, appeared with a railroad cap on and climbed the water tower and swung the water arm over the engine. The tall man waved to the man on the tower and he climbed down and connected the arm to the engine's water tank.

A cattle car door slid open and three men with rifles stood in the open doorway, looking at them. The tall man moved over to Rance and stopped just out of reach.

"I'm the engineer, name's Morgan. What you boys doin' here?"

"Lookin' for a ride to Texas," Rance said.

"We can get you to Pinefield, Arkansas. Have to catch another train to Texarkana from there. Looks like ya'll was in the war."

"Was," B.W. said. "Hear anything 'bout that actor killed Lincoln?"

"Federals killed him and goin' to hang some others for helpin' him."

"Good," B.W. said. "Wish it could have been me."

"Don't want no free ride," Rance said. "We can pay."

"Thought you might be goin' to rob us," Morgan said. "Takin' a load of beef to the army. Ten dollars and check those guns with me till we get there. Don't know if they got a car for your horses on the train out of Pinefield."

"Which one is that?" B.W. asked.

"Travers Southern Railway," Morgan said.

They looked at each other. "I'll be damned," B.W. said. "It is still runnin.'"

"We okay with this?" Rance said, looking at B.W. and Tommy.

"Don't think I want to give up my guns," B.W. said.

"That's the only way I'm goin' to do it," Morgan said. "Can't take any chances. You behave yourself, you'll get 'em back. Take a while to get to Pinefield."

"Don't have much choice, do we?" B.W. said.

"Nope," Morgan said.

"Guess we'll take it," Rance said. "Beats ridin' anyways."

"Alright, we'll drop a walk plank on the second car for the horses, nothing but calves in there,

shouldn't be any trouble. Give me the money and the guns when you get on. I'll give you a receipt for the money and weapons and we'll be on our way soon as the tank's full."

They untied the horses and led them into the cattle car. The calves backed up to give them room as they moved in. Morgan took their guns and money and handed Rance the receipt. He walked down the plank to the platform.

Two of the men with the rifles slid the walk plank in the car, closed the door and locked it. They could see them walk away through the railings.

"Be glad when we get there," B.W. said. "I feel naked without my guns and tomahawk."

"Not completely," Tommy said, and lifted Julie's Colt out of his saddle bags and handed it to B.W.

"Smart move, boy, adds some comfort."

The whistle blew, the engine moaned and black smoke drifted by the cattle cars as they pulled away. The rumbling sound of the locomotive got louder as it picked up speed. The train was soon at full-throttle, the locomotive churning out a stream of black smoke, the cattle cars bouncing and swaying.

B.W. and Rance stretched a lariat across a corner of the car and tied their horses to it to keep the calves off them and sat down in the corner. Tommy fell asleep as soon as he laid down.

After riding for hours the sun was long gone and the train moved deeper in to the night. The calves bellowed their displeasure and the horses stomped their feet every now and then. Shadows of trees and rocks whizzed by and the moon threw streaks of light through the railings into the cattle car.

Sometime in the early morning, they felt the train slowing down and saw the flicker of lights in the distance.

B.W. woke Tommy and they waited for the train to pull into the station.

When the train stopped, the engineer appeared and unlocked the car, and two of the guards opened the door and slid the walk plank in place. They led their horses out and then Morgan gave them back their weapons.

"This where we catch the train to Texas?" Rance asked.

"Passenger train but no cars for the horses," Morgan said. "Leaves at ten in the morning."

"No way to ship the horses?"

"Nope. Best you sell 'em. Livery will buy 'em. Get you some more when you get to Texas."

"I ain't sellin' my horse," Rance said. "I raised him from a colt and we survived a war together."

"Don't think I want to do that, either," B.W. said and Tommy also shook his head no.

"Long ride to Texas. Good luck. Got to let the army know we're here," Morgan said and walked away.

"Now what?" Tommy said

"Don't know," Rance said.

"Here, Tommy." B.W. handed him the Colt. "Put that back up, might need it again. " Tommy put the gun back in his saddle bags.

"Looks like town's just ahead," Rance said.

13

Willie Preston sold his horse, packed a bag and was sitting on a bench in front of the Wells Fargo stage office in Milberg with a bottle of whiskey, his shotgun propped against the wall next to him, waiting for the stage to arrive. Charlie Campbell came walking up to Preston and sat down on the bench beside him.

"Howdy, marshal," Charlie said.

"Ain't the marshal no more, Charlie."

"Yeah, I know. Habit, I guess. That's why I came to see you 'fore you left, tell you I was sorry for lettin' them get away."

"I'll find them."

"Colonel's got a man coming in from Abilene to replace you. Supposed to be here tomorrow."

"What's his name?" Preston said.

"Don't know. Don't really won't to work for anyone else anyway. Thought I might go with you. I got a score to settle with that one-arm Johnny Reb for taking my new Colt."

"Don't have enough money for the both us," Preston said.

"I got my own, I can carry my own weight."

"Don't have any authority anymore except as a bounty hunter. Most places think worse of bounty hunters than the outlaws."

"I know, but I want to go anyway," Charlie said. "Don't have no one here to hold me."

"Well, if you're hell-bent on goin' I could use the help," Preston said. "You got 'bout an hour 'fore the stage gets here to be ready. Gonna have to change stages three times and catch a train to Texas in Pinefield, Arkansas. It's a long ride, but better than a horse."

"You know whereabouts in Texas they went?" Charlie asked.

"Yeah, place called Traversville, 'bout fifty miles from Texarkana. That's where the boy's mama was from, accordin' to her former boss in Whiskey Gulch. They're takin' him home. I'm gonna beat 'em there."

"I'll get my things."

Charlie showed up as the stage was pulling in with a suitcase, a carbine and a Navy Colt.

The stage driver pulled the horses to a stop, jumped down and opened the door on the stage and held the hand of a pretty young lady as she stepped down.

The shotgun rider sat down his shotgun and helped her take her trunk off the stage. Preston and the other men followed her with their eyes as she sashayed down the street to the first saloon she came to and went in, the two men following with the trunk.

"Guess we know what her occupation is," Charlie said.

A man wearing a fancy suit and a bowler hat carrying a small carpet bag stepped down from the stage and walked over to Charlie.

"Where's the best place to stay around here?"

"Jack's Eatery down the street," Charlie said.

"Thanks." The man walked away carrying his bag.

"Another carpet bagger," Preston said and went back to sipping his whiskey.

The gruff-looking stage driver slapped his hat on his leg to shake the dust off of it then dusted himself off. He dipped his bandana in the water trough, wrung it out and wiped his sweaty face.

"Ain't you the marshal here?" he asked Preston.

"Not anymore," Preston said.

"You goin' on the stage?" He tugged his suspenders up to raise his sagging pants.

"We are," Preston said.

"They call me Patty. Glad to see you packin' them guns. We been runnin' into hostiles the last couple of times out, could use some more firepower."

"What kind of hostiles?"

"Mostly stray Creek war parties, usually four or five. Been able to fend them off so far but you never know when they may come at you with the whole damn tribe. We'll be ready to go after I change horses and get something to eat. We'll make a stop at Cally Springs for the night then just stop for horses and rest stops the rest of the way to Pinefield.

The stage driver climbed back up on the stage coach seat, tapped the reins on the six horses' backs and headed for the livery stable.

"You gonna kill 'em?" Charlie asked.

"Got to." Preston picked up the shotgun. "They're wanted for murder, got every right to. Ain't no two ways about it."

A chubby little woman wearing a red dress and matching hat with feathers on top came out of the saloon where the girl from the stage went in. She was hurrying down the street toward the stage office, carrying a purse and a carpet bag. She walked up to Preston and Charlie.

"Marshal, I want that floozy arrested." She pointed to a cut on her neck. "She tried to cut my throat! Told me to get out of town. Tried to kill me!"

"Looks like you been replaced, Shirley," Preston said and grinned. "Can't help you. Not the marshal no more. Me and Charlie are leaving town."

Shirley looked at Preston's shirt for the badge. "Well I'll be damned," she said. "Who's the marshal now?"

"Don't have one yet," Charlie said.

"Where you goin?" she asked.

"Pinefield," Preston said.

The shotgun rider came out of the stage office toting his shotgun and saddle bags. "What you doin' here, Shirley?"

"Go away," she said. "Buy me a ticket, Willie, for all those freebies I gave you."

"Can't afford it," Preston said.

"You owe me, marshal," she said, angrily.

"I'll buy you a ticket for a roll in the hay," Charlie said.

She looked at Charlie. "We'll, can't stay here," she said. "I'll pay up when we get to Pinefield."

Charlie smiled, took her bag and they walked in the office.

Preston shook his head. "One born every minute," he said.

"You ord'not let that bitch go," the shotgun rider said, holding the shotgun in the crook of his arm as he climbed into the seat.

"She ain't goin' to pay up. Charlie wasted his money," Preston said. "Another sucker."

The stage coach came rolling down the street with fresh horses and stopped in front of the stage office. Preston put his bag in the stage box and climbed in, laid the shotgun across his lap and took his whiskey bottle out of his coat pocket.

Charlie and Shirley came out of the office hand-in-hand, getting on the stage. Patty busted air with his whip and the horses took off. Charlie and Shirley snuggled up together on the other seat. Preston grinned.

14

Pinefield was the biggest town they had come to yet. Even in the wee hours of the morning the saloons were still alive and people were wandering the streets.

"Think they got any word here 'bout us breakin' out of jail?" Tommy said.

"Maybe," B.W. said. "Word gets around a lot quicker now with the telegraph."

"The skies are lightening up," Rance said. "Be sunrise soon. We'll move around easy-like, get some supplies and get out of town 'fore most folks start starin.'"

"I want some peppermint sticks," Tommy said.

"If they got 'em," Rance said.

"Let's find the livery and take care of the horses," B.W. said. "Might have to push 'em hard if the law gets after us."

A little further down the street they came to a livery stable with a sign on the door.

"What's that sign say?" Tommy asked.

"Say's they open at six," B.W. said.

"What time is it now?"

"Don't know," Rance said. "Use to have a watch till a Yankee sergeant at the hospital stole it."

"Or you lost it," B.W. said.

"He stole it. I know he did," Rance said. "My grandpa gave me that watch."

"Too bad," B.W. said. "From the looks of that glow in the east I would say it's five-thirty."

Rance glanced at the sky, tilted his head and looked at B.W. "Five-thirty, you sure 'bout that?"

"Pretty sure, yeah."

They rode up to the livery stable, dismounted and tied their horses to the hitching post.

"Think I'll partake of a little whiskey to warm the mornin' air," B.W. said. "Care to join me, major?"

"Too early for me."

"That stuff made me sick," Tommy said. "Don't think I ever want any again."

"For the best." B.W. reached in his saddle bags, took the whisky bottle out, screwed the cap off and took a big slug, shook his head, put the cap back on and put the bottle back in his saddle bags.

A few minutes later, the sun was peeking over the hills and a big man getting up in years showed up wearing a dirty black hat and scuffed boots. He had to be sixty-something. You could tell by the way he walked he knew his age.

"You boys here bright and early," he said. "What you want me to do with them horses?"

"Feed, water and and loosen the girths for a while while we get something to eat and some supplies," Rance said.

"Strangers, ain't you? Be five dollars for the care."

"Kinda high. That your strangers price?" B.W. said.

"Take it or leave it. I'm the only livery stable in town. Pay in advance."

"Check their shoes, too, we don't want one of 'em to throw one."

"I'll do it. Cost another dollar for the three."

B.W. shook his head and counted out the money. "That shotgun on my horse disappears, you'll pay for it. Where can we get some goods?"

"It'll be there. There's a store down the street to your left," he said. "You can get breakfast at the Emporium Saloon next door if you have a mind to."

They pulled the Henrys out of their saddle boots and looked up and down the street, saw a saloon with an Emporium sign and a mercantile store next to it.

"My gut tells me there's trouble here," B.W. said.

"Don't know 'bout your gut but the less contact we have here the better off we are," Rance said.

"Best we pick up what we need at the store and get back to the horses."

"Think so too," B.W. said.

They cradled the Henrys and headed to the store. When they walked in a mousy-looking little man with an apron was putting money in his register. He stopped and looked at them.

"What can I do for you?" he asked, glancing down behind the counter at a sawed-off shotgun.

"Just need a few things," Rance said. "And the boy wants some peppermint sticks."

"I'll get it for you and run a tally. Tell me your list."

"Okay," Rance said. "You got some oats?"

"Yep, fifty pound sacks in the back."

"Don't need that much," Rance said. "If you could put about twenty pounds in a gunny sack for us that would be good. Need some canned meats and beans, some beef jerky, coffee..."

"And peppermint sticks," Tommy said.

"You got ammo?" B.W. said.

"What you need?"

"Six boxes for the Henrys. Three boxes each for the .44 and .45 Colts. Two for a twelve-gauge."

"That's a lot of ammunition. Plan on startin' another war?" the man said and smiled.

"Might be," B.W. said with a frown and the clerk's smile disappeared faster than it came. He gathered the rest of the supplies and laid them on the counter.

Tommy spotted the peppermint sticks in a glass jar and took the top off and grabbed a handful and laid them on the counter beside the supplies. "You got any licorice?"

"We do."

"I'll take some of that, too," Tommy said.

The clerk picked up several sticks of licorice from a jar and showed them to Tommy.

"That enough?"

"Yes sir," Tommy said.

"Anything else?"

"That's it," Rance said. "How much we owe you?"

"Let me get your oats and I'll add it up." He came back with the oats and started ringing up the goods on his register. "Looks like eight-fifty."

B.W. pulled a ten dollar gold piece out of his pocket and handed it to the clerk.

"Ain't seen one of those for a while." He put the gold piece in the register, handed B.W. his change and closed the register. He put everything in sacks and they picked up the supplies and headed for the door.

Three men stepped into the doorway with tin stars on their shirts, pointing rifles at them with six-shooters hanging on their hips. The man in the middle wore a sheriff's badge and the other two men deputy badges. They were all young, the sheriff the oldest. The one on his left was stocky, freckled-face with red hair. The one on the right was shorter, heavier, wearing a straw hat and knee-high boots, his pants stuffed in his boots. Probably more sod buster than deputy. The sheriff was the neater and slimmer of the three, with a white Stetson on his head, brown eyes and a neatly-trimmed black mustache.

"Looks like they knew we were coming," Rance said.

"Yeah, got us cold," B.W. said.

"I'm Sheriff Russell Brim and these men are my deputies, Red and Bobby. You're under arrest for robbing our bank. Put your weapons on the floor and step away from them."

Rance, B.W. and Tommy looked at each other. "Did he say bank?" Tommy asked.

"Did you say we robbed a bank?" Rance said.

"Yep, now put them guns on the floor like I told you," Brim said.

Rance and B.W. sat the goods down then laid the rifles and Colts on the floor beside them.

The store clerk lifted the sawed off shotgun from under the counter, pointing it at them.

"The tomahawk too," Brim said.

B.W. slid his hand under his tomahawk and looked at Rance.

Rance shook his head no and B.W. laid the tomahawk on the floor.

"Witnesses saw you ride out of town last night on a buckskin and a big black after you blew the bank safe. They couldn't see you straight up but you got the same profile."

"Sheriff," B.W. said. "You got the wrong men. We been ridin' a train all night. Got into town just a couple hours ago."

"You're lyin'," Brim said. "Red here saw you talkin' to the smith this mornin' holdin' them same horses."

"We brought the horses in on the train. Not the horses you're talkin' about," Rance said. "We got a receipt."

"A load of cattle for the army did come in this mornin'," Red said. Bobby nodded in agreement.

"Let's see that receipt," Brim said. "Red, check their saddle bags."

Red lowered his rifle and walked out the door.

"What's in those saddle bags is ours," B.W. said.

"I've got to get the receipt out of my pocket," Rance said. "Don't anybody get an itchy trigger finger." He reached in his pocket, took out the receipt and handed it to the sheriff.

Sheriff Brim looked at the receipt. "Where'd you get them horses?"

"Raised mine," Rance said.

"I picked mine up on the battlefield when his rider was shot off him at Gettysburg," B.W. said.

Rance looked at B.W. He didn't know that.

"What about the boy?" Brim asked.

"That's another story. You said it was two men," Rance said. He makes three.

Red came back in shaking his head. "Got some money but not enough to be the banks,'" he
said.

"Most of the cash from the bank was paper money the Yankees just brought in. Southern money ain't really worth a shit right now," Brim said. "Maybe we do have the wrong men. Be awful stupid for you to come back if it was. Hell of a thing, though, same kind of horses and all. Guess we'll have to form a posse, see if the bank wants to put up a reward."

"Then we can go?" Rance asked.

"Yeah, pick up your gear and be on your way," Brim said. They lowered the rifles, turned and walked out of the store. The clerk let the hammers down on his shotgun and put it back under the counter. "Sorry boys, the war has brought a lot of bad people our way."

Rance and B.W. picked up their things, left the store, stopped at the emporium, picked up a batch of biscuits and walked back to the livery stable.

"Can you believe that?" Rance said, looking at B.W.

"Nope."

"Me neither," Tommy said. "They don't know 'bout us."

They paid the blacksmith and divided the biscuits, B.W. getting two more than Rance and Tommy.

They gathered their horses and gear and rode out easy-like, Tommy chewing on a peppermint stick.

"You know," B.W. said, "it just occurred to me. The bank wasn't the only one robbed. I think that deputy stole two ten-dollar gold pieces. Noticed they was gone when I paid the smith."

"You sure?" Rance said.

"Yeah, that sonofabitch stole our money."

"Well we ain't goin' back," Rance said. "May not get out of there again. We were lucky the first time. Let him keep it."

"Wonder where those bank robbers went," B.W. said.

"No way," Rance said. "If you're thinkin' 'bout robbin' the robbers you can forget it. We're goin' to Texas."

"Bet we could take 'em."

Rance looked away and kept riding.

15

They put a ride on and got several miles away as fast as they could before they slowed down to let their horses lumber along across a green meadow, snipping the moist grass as they moved along.

"Is this pretty country or what," B.W. said, his horse's reins wrapped around the saddle horn taking a drink of whiskey and a bite of a biscuit.

"Think we can relax a little now?" Tommy asked.

"That train ride left Marshal Preston a long way behind, if he's still comin' that is," B.W. said.

"Unless he caught a train, too," Rance said. "You thought out how we're goin' about Tommy's problem when we get to Texas?"

"If you mean the law, no," B.W. said. "Have to get a license to practice there so it may not matter anyway. May have to figure something else out."

"I don't care what you do," Tommy said.

"Probably just as well. He's not goin' to share his fortune with a kid he hasn't seen since he was a baby, regardless of what a court says. May have to kill the sonofabitch," B.W. said.

"No-never-mind to me," Tommy said.

"You never intended to go to court with this did you?" Rance said. "We should have had this talk before we started."

"Meaning what?" B.W. said.

"Meaning we ain't no better than he is if we don't do this right. We're nothin' but outlaws."

"Guess you could say that. You sound like you're thinkin' about what you're goin' to get out of it."

"Didn't come for the money," Rance said. "Trying to help the boy, that's all."

The cracking sound of a rifle shot echoed across the meadow and clipped B.W.'s whiskey bottle, breaking it into a thousand pieces. They saw gun smoke rush out of a pine grove tree line.

"Run!" Rance said as he spurred Buck and he was at a full gallop in two strides with B.W. and Tommy close behind.

They rode into a small group of cottonwoods along a creek bank, dismounted, grabbed the Henrys from the saddle boots and hit the ground.

"What'a we do?" Tommy said.

"Wait and see who's out there," B.W. said.

A bullet slammed into a cottonwood just above B.W.'s head and two riders rode out of a thicket like the devil was after them, firing their pistols.

B.W. knocked the lead rider off his horse with his first shot some twenty yards away and Rance picked off the other one.

The riderless horses galloped on toward them then turned and trotted off several yards away. One was a buckskin and the other one a black.

When no more riders appeared. Rance took the spyglass off his saddle and scanned the trees but didn't see anyone else. They walked out to the men on the ground, leading their horses. B.W. rolled one of them over on his back. He was dead. He didn't look much older than Tommy.

"I'll be damned," B.W. said. "It's a kid."

Rance checked the other one. "This one too."

"Was awful dumb for them to charge like that," B.W. said. "Had to kill 'em."

"Couldn't be more than fifteen," Rance said. "Got on rebel pants and boots, might have been in the war. You notice the horses?"

"Yeah, looks like we found the bank robbers. Too bad we had to kill 'em."

"Must have thought we were the posse."

"Would think so."

"Kids. Why would they rob a bank?"

"For the money, I imagine."

"You know what I mean. Kids!" Rance said. "They probably didn't even have a family."

"Guess we'll never know," B.W. said. "I'll check the horses."

"I'll see what the boys have on them," Rance said.

Both looked like they had been wearing the same clothes for a while. One of them had a small pocket knife and the other one two aggie marbles and some gold coins in his pants pockets. They had pictures inside their hat brims of a middle-aged man in a Confederate uniform with a woman about the same age standing beside him. Rance compared the pictures, they were the same. Must have been brothers.

B.W. appeared leading the boys' horses. "These horses got four bags of money in the saddle bags from Pinefield State Bank," he said. "Maybe fifteen or twenty-thousand dollars in them bags. Lots of federal paper money, some gold and silver coins, too. We're rich if that federal money is good."

"It's bad money. We would be bank robbers," Rance said. "We have to give it back."

"Are you crazy?" B.W. said. "No way."

"It's wrong, can't you see that?"

"What did I ever do for a conscience 'fore I met you," B.W. said.

"May not have had one," Rance said.

"Oh I have one, I just don't get carried away with it like you do," B.W. said. "Do you think anyone else in their right mind would give back that much money in these kind of times?"

"Guess we just have a different view of what's right and wrong."

"Don't I get a say in this?" Tommy said.

"Yes you do, partner," B.W. said. "Let's hear it."

"I think the major's right," Tommy said. "We don't need another posse after us."

B.W. stared at Tommy "You stole pennies and dimes from Harden," B.W. said. "Now you're wantin' to give up a fortune too?"

"That's what we have to do," Rance said. "May be a town is close by. Take the money and the kids there and have them notify the sheriff in Pinefield. Don't want to backtrack, may run into Preston."

"What if I say no?" B.W. said.

"Then I'll do it anyway," Rance said.

"You that set on this?" B.W. said.

"Yeah," Rance said. "Let's head out. Keep movin' south while we still got daylight."

"If we run into any of their kin we may have to kill some more of that family," B.W. said. "What's your conscience say about that, major?"

"Won't change what we got to do with the money, whatever happens."

"I could just take the money and leave," B.W. said.

"Couldn't let you do that," Rance said.

"You know you would have to kill me."

"I do."

"Or I would have to kill you first."

"You would," Rance said.

"Damn it, I can't go against you both. I don't like it, but okay. We better do it soon, them bodies are gonna start stinking."

"We'll find a town that'll bury 'em," Rance said.

"That's right considerate of you," B.W. said. "Since I won't have to do the digging."

They tied the dead boys on their horses and mounted. The lingering gun smoke disappeared in the trees from a cross wind as they rode away.

Further down the trail, they saw a sign reading Buffalo Flats — Four Miles. They stopped and looked at the sign.

"If they got a road sign it's probably big enough to have a telegraph," Rance said.

"Maybe," B.W. said. "Didn't that sheriff say he was going to see if the bank would put up a reward?"

"Seems like I recall that," Rance said.

"Maybe we won't come out of this too bad after all," B.W. said.

"Unless they know somebody's after us," Tommy said.

16

Everyone stared at the dead boys as they rode down the street. Soldiers from both sides, still in uniform, some missing arms and legs, standing around doing nothing.

By the time they got to the sheriff's office they had gathered a motley-looking crowd of ex-soldiers and old men.

They rode up to the sheriff's office. Rance dismounted and tied Buck to the hitching post.

"Might be better if you and Tommy stay on your horses while I check in with the sheriff," Rance said.

B.W. nodded and took the lead rope from their horses.

"These people act like they never seen a dead man before," Tommy said.

"They seen plenty, just curious," B.W. said. "They think we might have somebody they know."

Someone in the crowd yelled, "Who you got?" as Rance walked into the sheriff's office.

A wiry-looking little man with sky blue eyes wearing a rebel hat stood up. He had a homemade tin star pinned on the black and white checked shirt he was wearing, and an ivory-handled Navy Colt hanging from his hip.

"What's all the commotion goin' on outside?" he asked.

"Got two dead ones outside. Bank robbers," Rance said. "You the sheriff?"

"I am. Name's Sheriff Billy Shaw. You bounty hunters?"

"No," Rance said.

"How you know they robbed a bank?"

"We heard about it when we was in Pinefield. Money bags had Pinefield Bank on them, money was still in the bags. They charged us on the trail, thinking we were the posse, I guess. Didn't have a choice but to kill or be killed. Just kids, though, hate that it had to happen."

"You don't say," he said. "You have this money with you?"

"We do, in their saddle bags out front."

"Who's we?"

"An Indian and a boy I'm ridin' with."

"Let's have a look." The sheriff stood up and headed for the door. Rance followed.

"Alright," the sheriff said to the crowd. "You boys go on, this is law business."

An old skinny man with a long white beard and a face full of wrinkles stepped in front of the sheriff.

"Who they got, sheriff?" he asked.

"None of your business, Welford, now move out the way." The sheriff pushed the old man aside, grabbed the hair of one of the dead boys hanging across his horse and raised his head. "Know him," he said. "Ike Bannister."

He dropped the boy's head and repeated the same thing with the other one. "This is his bother, Keavy. The Bannisters lived on a small farm outside of town. Was the only ones left from a Yankee raid on their farm last winter. Bring those saddle bags in and let's have a look. Welford, take these boys to the undertaker for me. Tell him we'll settle up with him later."

"Do I get any whiskey money out of it?" the old man asked.

The sheriff handed Welford a coin.

B.W. and Tommy dismounted, tied the horses to the hitching post, got the saddle bags and handed Welford the reins to the dead boys' horses and he led them away.

B.W. and Tommy sat the saddle bags beside the desk and the sheriff opened them and took the bank bags out and placed them on the desk.

"Like you said, got Pinefield Bank painted on the bags." He opened one of the bank bags, scooped a handful of gold coins and some paper money out and laid it on the desk. "Lot of money here."

"There is," B.W. said and gave Rance a hard look.

"Said those boys attacked you?" the sheriff said.

"Came charging out of a thicket, shootin' at us," B.W. said. "Didn't have a choice but to shoot back."

"Known them boys all their life. They was having a hard time makin' it."

"The war has made it hard for all of us," Rance said.

"You lose that arm in the war?" Sheriff Shaw asked.

"I did."

"He was a rebel major," Tommy said.

"What 'bout you," Shaw said, looking at B.W.

"Was on the winnin' side," B.W. said.

Shaw looked at B.W. with a cold stare for several seconds and B.W. returned it.

"You got any deputies?" Rance asked.

"Not yet," he said. "Mayor appointed me sheriff two weeks ago. May not be able to pay me unless the Yankees fork over some money."

"You got a bank?" Rance said.

"No, went belly up some time ago."

"Got anyone to help you look after that money you can trust?" B.W. said.

"Just me. That's it."

"Is there a telegraph to let the sheriff in Pinefield know what happened?" Rance said. "So they can come get their money."

"We got a telegraph at the train station."

"You got a train runnin' out of here?" Rance said, surprised.

"Yep, twice a week. One going south on Tuesday, one going north on Saturday."

"That's tomorrow," B.W. said. "The one going south headed to Texas?"

"Think so," Shaw said. "You thinkin' 'bout catchin' it?"

"Maybe," B.W. said. "Is there a livery stable and a place to eat in this town?"

"On down the street. Livery's 'fore you get to the Chinaman's café."

"I see you got a safe," Rance said.

"We'll have to count it," Billy said. "Need a witness on how much is there 'fore I put it in the safe."

"Don't know if they spent any," Rance said. "We haven't touched it."

"Major, how 'bout you and Tommy go take care of the horses and eat," B.W. said. "I'll help him count the money and put it in the safe. I'd like to know how much is there, too. Bring me some biscuits and whiskey."

Shaw looked at B.W. with a strange expression. "Biscuits and whiskey?"

"Good," B.W. said.

Shaw shook his head. "Okay, I'll give the undertaker their horses for burying 'em since there's no one to claim 'em."

"That okay,?" Rance said, looking at B.W. and Tommy.

"One oughta do it," B.W. said. "Think the sheriff should have one for takin' care of the money."

Rance and Tommy nodded in agreement.

"Appreciate that," Shaw said. "Comin' from a Indian Yankee."

B.W. grinned.

"Okay, we'll be back in a little while," Rance said. "B.W., you make sure none of that money disappears."

"Don't forget the whiskey," B.W. said.

"And biscuits," Rance said and left.

When Rance and Tommy returned, they brought B.W. the whiskey and biscuits and sat them on the desk.

"Thanks," B.W. said. "We counted the money. Twenty-one-thousand, eight-hundred dollars and ninety-six cents. Sixteen thousand in paper money, the rest in gold and silver coins. He gave me a receipt."

"I'll go send the telegram to the sheriff in Pinefield and wait for a reply," Shaw said.

"What time that train leave for Texas?" Rance asked.

"Tomorrow morning, ten-o'clock," Shaw said. "The Fast Hitch Saloon has beds, fifty cents. Can come by there, let you know what the Pinefield sheriff said when I hear back."

"Just as soon you didn't say anything 'bout us in that telegram," Rance said. "Just tell him 'bout the boys and the money."

"What if there's a reward?" Shaw said.

"We'll take it out of the bank money," B.W. said.

"I'll handle it right now," Shaw said.

"Good. Find out if we can ship our horses too," Rance said and they walked back outside.

"Don't think I want to sleep in a bed," B.W. said. "Somethin' bad always happens when I do."

"That's ridiculous, just a coincidence," Rance said.

"Don't think so."

"That's silly," Tommy said. Rance nodded.

"Alright, but I warned you," B.W. said and they walked across the street into the saloon.

A big-headed man with almost as much hair on his eyebrows as his head and a salt-and-pepper beard watched them come in and walk up to the bar. He looked at Tommy and shook his head.

"Don't allow no kids in here," he said.

"We just want a bed for the night, nothing else," Rance said. "Got a train to catch in the mornin.'"

"Don't matter. No kids in here."

"Just as well," B.W. said. "Didn't want to stay here anyway."

"You're not goin' to rent us a bed?" Rance asked.

"Not with the kid," the man said. "My place, my rules."

"Give it up, major, we'll sleep in the livery," B.W. said. "Would feel better there, anyway."

"Let's go," Rance said and they walked back out on the street. "We'll wait for the sheriff then go to the livery stable. Guess sleepin' on hay don't count as a bed, huh, B.W.?"

"Nope." B.W. sat down on the board sidewalk and stretched his long legs out in front of him.

When the sheriff showed up they were leaning against the wall, half asleep.

"How come you're not inside?" Shaw asked.

"Wouldn't rent us a bed with the boy," Rance said.

"Wait here, I'll take care of it. Solomon can be a cantankerous old cuss sometimes."

"It's alright, B.W. don't want to sleep in a bed anyway," Rance said.

"How come?"

"It's a long story," Tommy said.

"What did Pinefield say?" Rance asked.

"They're gonna catch the next train to pick up the money," Shaw said. "Bank put up a five-hundred-dollar reward for the return of the money."

"Anyone beside the telegrapher know about the money?" Rance asked.

"No."

"Keep it that way," B.W. said. "That's a big temptation for anyone."

"Sure is," the sheriff said.

"Think we better move on," Rance said. "If they got a place for our horses on that train in the mornin."

"Asked them 'bout that," Shaw said. "The one comin' tomorrow is a cattle car, said you can take your horses."

"Then that's what we'll do," Rance said.

"Sheriff," B.W. said. "Think we'll take that five-hundred now unless you've got some objections."

"And if I did?" he asked.

"We'll, we'd have take it anyway," B.W. placed his hand on the butt of his Colt.

"I'll tell them when they get here," Shaw said.

B.W. collected the five hundred, gave Billy a hundred for his trouble and they spent the night in the livery stable, sleeping on hay — much to B.W.'s satisfaction.

17

They were up early, saddling their horses when they heard a train whistle.

"The train's here," B.W. said. "It's a little after seven."

"We better high-tail it out there," Rance said and they hurried outside to see tumbleweeds rolling down the street from a gusting wind. They hung on to their hats, mounted and took off.

The train was pulling out from the station as they rode up with their hats in their hands. They tied their horses to a hitching post and the horses turned sideways from the wind. The train blew its whistle as it crossed a dirt road on the edge of town. The horses started prancing around the station agent walking toward them. He looked like a ghost with his tall, thin frame, swinging the glowing lantern, his snow white hair and beard blowing in the early morning wind.

"Hey!" B.W. yelled. "How come the train's leaving early?"

The man stopped and waited for them to get closer. "What's that you say?" he asked. "Couldn't hear you with the whistle blowing."

"Why is the train leaving early?" Rance said.

"Leaving on time," the man said.

"Thought it didn't leave until ten?"

"Nope, seven-thirty like always." He raised the globe on his lantern and the wind blew it out.

"Where's the cattle cars?" B.W. said.

"It's a passenger train, don't no pull cattle."

"Did Sheriff Shaw send a telegram to Pinefield yesterday?" Rance asked.

"Nope. Would have had me do it. I'm the only one knows how."

"Should have asked for a copy of the telegram," Rance said.

"He was formulatin' this from the time he saw the money," B.W. said. "I could see it in his eyes, thought if I gave him the horse and money it would ease the temptation. Shaw's on that train, ain't he?"

"He is," the agent said. "Said he quit and was goin' to California. Seemed all excited, kept lookin' over his shoulder like he was expectin' someone."

"He was," Rance said "We're here."

"Wish I had listened to B.W. now," Tommy said. " No way we can catch up. He's long gone."

"Me too," Rance said.

"Got a leak in the boiler," the agent said. "They're goin' to have to fix it when they get to Hudsonville. Got no tools here, probably take all day."

"How far is that from here?" Rance asked.

"Twenty miles or so."

"What's the quickest way?"

"Follow the tracks, pretty straight shot from here," the agent said. "Tried to tell him but he was too jumpy to listen."

"Thanks," Rance said and they hurried to the horses. They rode hard until their horses started puffing and stopped to rest them. They dismounted and wet the horses' noses from their canteens.

"We gonna kill him?" Tommy said.

"Don't know yet," B.W. said.

"What you think, major?" Tommy said.

"I'll let B.W. make the call."

"I know what you was thinkin' but everything has changed," B.W. said. "It's dog-eat-dog now and it's goin' to be that way for a long time."

Rance didn't say anything, just grabbed the saddle horn with his good hand and pulled himself up in the saddle. They rode another mile or two and came over a rise and saw the train in the distance, sitting at a depot on the outskirts of town, men working on the train's engine.

"There it is," B.W. said. "He may have figured out we're coming and is already gone. He damn sure had money to buy a horse."

They rode down a long slope across an open field of blue bonnets, crossed the tracks and stopped near a big man wearing overalls with a railroad cap on his bushy hair, a huge hand wrapped around the handle of a sledgehammer resting on the ground. Three Chinese men were working on the train. The big man wasn't carrying a gun but a rifle was propped against a tree some ten feet away.

"Any of the passengers still on the train?" Rance said.

"Who the hell are you?" the man asked.

"Someone that will ask you a question if you don't mind," B.W. said.

"Unless you got someone on the train or you're the law, I ain't got time for you."

"Not very friendly, are you?" Tommy said.

"And you don't know how to respect your elders, do you boy?"

B.W. rode up between the man and the rifle, slid off his horse and wrapped the reins around the saddle horn.

The three men working on the engine stopped and looked at what was going on.

The big man picked up the hammer, back-peddled to the steps of the passenger car, took a firm grip on the handle of the sledgehammer with both hands. "You're not goin' on this train."

"Get out of my way," B.W. said and started walking toward him.

"Over my dead body," the man said.

"That can be arranged." B.W. jerked the tomahawk from his belt and hurled it toward the man, cutting off two fingers from his right hand. The man yelled in pain. The sledgehammer fell to the ground along with his two fingers, the tomahawk stuck in the handle. He dropped to his knees and grabbed his bleeding hand, looking at his fingers on the ground between his knees.

"You fuckin' red nigger, I'll kill you!"

"Not today," B.W. said and drew his Colt.

"Let it go," Rance yelled. "Check the train, I'll take care of him."

B.W. stared at Rance for a second, stuck the Colt back in his belt, picked up the sledgehammer beside the wounded man, pulled the bloody tomahawk out of the handle, wiped it off on the back of the man's shirt, dropped the hammer, stuck the tomahawk in his belt and boarded the train. The three working men dropped their tools and took off running down the track.

"Where they goin?" Tommy said.

"They don't want no part of that tomahawk." Rance dropped down from his horse and walked up to the man.

"You goin' to shoot me?"

"You don't know how close you came to dying just then," Rance said. "He could have put that tomahawk between your eyes. I know. I've seen him do it before."

The man pulled a bandana from around his neck with his left hand and wrapped his wounded one with it. "Who are you lookin for?" he said, grimacing in pain.

"Wanted to know if Sheriff Billy Shaw was on the train."

"I don't know. Wagons took them all to town to eat a while ago."

"How long?"

"Couple of hours, tops."

"When's this train going to be ready to go?"

"Don't know that either, you ran my workers off and mangled me."

"Where does it stop next?"

"Go to hell," he said.

"You'll proably be there to greet us," Rance said.

B.W. stepped off the train. "Nobody on it."

"I know, he just told me," Rance said. "Wagons took them all to town."

B.W. glanced at the man, walked to his horse, unwrapped the reins from the saddle horn and climbed on.

"Better get that treated soon," Rance said to the man and held up his handless arm up for him to see.

Tommy rode up leading Buck and held the reins while Rance climbed on and they headed for town with B. W

They saw a bunch of people climbing into the wagons to return to the train as they rode in. Billy wasn't one of them.

"Most likely he's gone," B.W. said. "He knows we would be on his trail. Let's check the livery stable, see if he bought a horse."

They rode down the street until they saw the livery stable and rode up to the open door. Just inside the door, a man wearing a rebel hat with a wooden leg was dipping a hot horseshoe in a water trough, steam bellowing up. They dismounted and led their horses up to the man.

"Howdy," Rance said. The man laid the horseshoe on an anvil, set the tongs down and leaned against the horse he was shoeing.

"Howdy," he said.

"We're looking for a little man with blue eyes, may be wearing a rebel hat like yours with an ivory-handled Colt. Wondered if you seen him?"

"Nope, ain't been here," the man said. He looked at Rance. "You too, huh?"

"'Fraid so, Forty-First Virginia," Rance said.

"Was with Jeb Stuart when he went down. Name's Mackey. What you want that fella for?"

"Kind of personal," Rance said.

Mackey nodded.

"Maybe he stole a horse," B.W. said, looking at Rance and Tommy.

"What do we do now?" Tommy said.

"Don't know," B.W. said. "Have a look around town, I guess, might be in one of the saloons."

"Thanks for your time," Rance said, looking at Mackey.

He nodded again and picked up the tongs.

They mounted, turned around and rode up to a saloon and dismounted. "Hold the horses," B.W. said and handed the reins to Tommy.

Two rough-looking cowboys standing at the bar drinking whiskey with middle-aged, worn-out-looking whores were the only ones in the place except for the bartender. He was fat and red-eyed. He looked like he might be his own best customer. He wiped his bloodshot eyes and leaned on the bar.

"What'll you have," he said.

"Just lookin' for someone, won't be long," Rance said.

"You ain't buyin' nothin?'"

"Not now," Rance said. "Let's go."

"Good advice," the bartender said as they walked out on the street.

"Now what?" B.W. said.

"Beats me. No tellin' where he is," Rance said.

A Wells Fargo stagecoach came rolling by. They looked at the stagecoach then each other.

"Billy," Rance said big-eyed.

They hurried to their horses, climbed on and took off after the stage coach.

B.W. galloped up beside the moving stagecoach, tied the reins on the saddle horn as he galloped along, grabbed the door, lifted his feet out of the stirrups and pulled himself inside the stage through the door window into Billy's lap. Billy went for his gun but B.W. hit him as hard as he could with his fist, grabbing Billy's gun and throwing it out the window, then drew his Colt and stuck it under Billy's chin.

Two spinsters on the opposite seat with frilly dresses, strapped sack purses hanging on their arms and bonnets on, broke into a screaming duet and put each other in a bear hug.

"Shut up!" B.W. yelled and they turned the screams off and tightened their grip on each other, shaking like a wind-blown leaf.

B.W.'s big black was running alongside the stage horses. "Looky there, Shorty," the driver said. "Where's his rider?"

Shorty turned and looked behind them. "Two riders comin', Zeb!" Shorty yelled. "The other one must be inside."

Zeb wrapped his hands around the reins and started reining the horses in and came to a stop. They jumped down from the seat with their shotguns. Zeb had his shotgun pointed at Rance and Tommy as they rode up and Shorty on the ground with his.

"Rein them horses in and drop your guns," Zeb said. "And get down off them horses."

"You in the stage coach, throw your guns out," Shorty said.

Rance dropped his guns on the ground and he and Tommy dismounted, holding the reins of their horses. Tommy stepped back from his saddle and leaned on his saddle bags. Zeb was waving the shotgun around like he may start shooting any time.

"Keep still, Tommy," Rance said.

"Throw your guns out now," Shorty said, looking at the stage.

"What if I keep 'em and hold on to these nice ladies?" B.W. said.

"Don't care," Zeb said. "I'll shoot you anyway."

"Did you hear that, Ethel?" one of the ladies said.

"I did, Sadie," the other one said. "He doesn't care if this savage kills us."

"Alright," B.W. said and tossed his Colt out and stuck his tomahawk in the back of his belt.

"All of you, get out," Zeb said.

"Get out, Billy," B.W. said.

"He means you too," Billy said.

Billy grabbed for his saddle bags and B.W. shoved his hand away and pushed him out the door and he followed, leaving the saddle bags on the stage. He turned back to the ladies to help them out but they wouldn't take his hand.

"Don't touch me, you savage," Ethel said and helped Sadie off the stage.

"He's got a tomahawk stuck in the back of his belt," Billy said.

"Put it on the ground, Injun," Zeb said.

B.W. pulled the tomahawk from his belt and dropped it on the ground.

"What're you doin' on my stage?" Zeb asked.

"Was catchin' up to this hombre," B.W. said, looking at Billy. "He stole our money."

"That right?" Zeb said, looking at Billy.

"No. I'm the sheriff of Buffalo Flats. They stole the money from the Pinefield Bank in Arkansas. I was takin' it back."

"Well if you were, you're goin' the wrong way," Zeb said.

"Was trying to throw them off my trail and double back," Billy said.

"Don't see no badge," Zeb said.

"That's 'cause he quit and ran off with the money," B.W. said. "We got it from the bank robbers and left it with him for the bank it came from, then found out he took off with it."

"This gets more confusing by the minute," Zeb said. "Guess I'll have to tie you up and sort this out when we get to Daring."

"You going to tie us up, too?" Sadie said. There was something in her voice that made it sound like she might enjoy it.

146

"No ma'am," Shorty said.

She looked at her companion and sighed.

Tommy eased his hand into his saddle bags and quickly removed the Colt and held it beside his leg.

He took a step towards Zeb. When the two men kept looking at the ladies, Tommy took another step behind Zeb and stuck the Colt to the back of his head.

"Put your shotguns down or I'll blow a hole in you both," Tommy said.

"He means it," B.W. said. "Drop 'em."

Zeb dropped his shotgun, then Shorty. Billy made a run for Shorty's shotgun and B.W. tripped him, stepped on his hand and he let out a yell.

"Damn that hurt!" Billy said.

"Was supposed to," B.W. said.

B.W. picked up Shorty's shotgun and Rance Zeb's.

"Now what," Zeb said.

"Nothin' unless you give us a reason," B.W. said. "Ladies, get on the stage and Billy, you stay right where you are." B.W. opened the stage door and picked up Billy's saddle bags off the seat. "Guess you ladies don't cotton to Indians so you can get on by yourself."

The two ladies helped each other back on the stage, sat down and Sadie stuck her arm out the window, shaking her fist at B.W. "The law's gonna get you!" she yelled.

"Pray for me," B.W. said and grinned.

"You can take your stage out of here if you keep going," Rance said. "Billy stays with us."

"Might need them shotguns. Indians and such," Zeb said and looked at B.W.

"I'll put them in the stage, you can stop and get them later," Rance said. "But it better be a long ways from here."

"Or this Indian will scalp you," B.W. said.

Zeb and Shorty swallowed hard climbed up on the seat and Zeb picked up the reins. The horses' harnesses rattled as he pulled the reins tight and they started off in a walk. Zeb cracked the whip over their heads. They broke into a gallop and were gone.

Tommy came riding up with B.W.'s horse and handed him the reins. B.W. held on to the reins and took the saddle bags off his arm and looked in.

"Looks like most of it's still here." He put the saddle bags on his horse's neck where he could see them.

"What're we goin' to do with him?" Tommy said.

"Well," B.W. said, "we got the money back, no sense killin' him now. Billy, it's not very far back to town. You can walk, buy you a horse and go on to California. Your gun is somewhere back on the trail."

"Got no reason to go now," Billy said.

"Better go to save your ass. If I ever see you again, I'll kill you," B.W. said.

"I know when it's over." Billy turned to the road, looked back and waved at B.W. and walked away, backtracking on the road to Buffalo Flats.

B.W. mounted his horse, Rance and Tommy followed. They rode away, Billy watching as they topped a hill and disappeared.

"Son of a bitch!" Billy yelled at the empty road and set out walking back to town, looking for the ivory-handled Navy Colt.

18

The horses were beginning to drop their head and walk slower. Time for a stop.

They found a small creek further down the trail, washed up, unsaddled their horses, gave them some oats and tied them to a tree limb. They laid their weapons on the saddles, started a fire and put a pot of beans on and settled down for some rest. As usual, Rance handed out the orders for the night. He placed his coffee cup on his notepad to hold it down and started writing in it. B.W. got his whiskey from Tommy's saddle bags and laid the money bags down beside him.

"What're you writing, major?" Tommy said.

"The ABCs."

"What's that?"

"The ABCs, the alphabet. You have to learn how to read letters before you can read words. After I get them on paper we'll start with four letters at a time until you know the alphabet."

"Boy, I wish I had some biscuits," B.W. said to himself, looking around like they would magically appear.

Rance and Tommy looked at B.W. and then each other and went back to talking.

"After we eat some beans we'll start," Rance said. "It all kind of comes together. If you learn to read, you can learn to write."

Rance showed Tommy the letters and had him repeat them several times, then put TOMMY together for him to study his name.

"Beans be ready after a while, B.W. You want any?" Rance said.

"Don't want no beans, want some biscuits," B.W. said. He sipped his whiskey while Rance and Tommy cooked their beans, Rance teaching him the alphabet. For over an hour.

"Beans are done, sure you don't want none?" Rance said.

"Naw, don't think so," B.W. said.

"You been sucking on that bottle for the last hour like it was your mama's tit," Rance said. "You're drunk. We have any trouble you wouldn't be worth a damn tonight."

"Could kick your one-armed ass," B.W. said.

"You are drunk," Tommy said.

"Young man, I'll decide what I am, not you," B.W. said and turned the whiskey bottle up for the last swallow in the bottle. He dropped his empty bottle and fell over on his saddle asleep.

"Guess he don't get no beans," Tommy said. "I'm goimng to pour out what's left. B.W. got anymore whiskey?"

"Don't know," Rance said. "No harm in havin' a drink every now and then but some folks don't know when to stop, and B.W. is one of them."

"Hope he don't have anymore," Tommy said.

"He'll get more," Rance said. "He'll wake up, feel bad 'bout it and cut down for a while, then do it all again. Some people can drink and some can't. My pa was a lot like B.W. Didn't know when to put the bottle down. It's why I watch myself with the whiskey."

"How do you know if you can't?" Tommy said.

"You don't. Every time we stop for the rest of the way I'll teach you more. By the time we get to Texas you should be readin' some and writin' a little."

"What do you think my pa will do when he sees me?"

"Well, I don't think he's goin' to welcome you with open arms or he wouldn't have sent you away to start with. If he had anything to do with your mama bein' murdered then that's a whole different story."

"You think he did?"

"If we can find the cowboy with the fancy boots we might know."

"We got money now, why don't we just go someplace and buy us a ranch and forget about Texas?"

"Might consider that."

"What if I don't want to go to Texas?" Tommy said.

"Then maybe we buy that ranch."

"I'll think on it."

"You do that," Rance said, "now let's get some shut eye."

B.W. sat up, picked up his empty whiskey bottle, squinted his eyes and looked in it, dropped it and eased back down on his saddle and closed his eyes.

An owl got an early start on the night and a wolf's howl in the distance made the horses uneasy.

Rance picked up his Henry, checked it and his double-action Colt and sat back down against an oak.

Tommy sat down beside him. "What if Billy gets a horse and shows up?"

"He won't. He knows better."

"I been thinkin,'" Tommy said. "You said you thought the man that murdered my mama may be from Texas. Made up my mind. I want to go to Texas and kill that sonofabitch. She may have been a whore but she was a good mama and took good care of me."

"Leave the cussin' to B.W. like he said. Nothin' says we'll find him but we can try."

Tommy laid down on his saddle.

Rance looked up at the star-filled sky, it always made him think of Paige and his daughter. Taking care of Tommy made the pain a little more bearable and he fell asleep.

As the morning sunlight tiptoed through the trees to the creek, he got up to build a fire to fix coffee. B.W. sat up and made a horrible face, rubbed his head, picked up his Henry and used it to get to his feet. He saw the coffee pot on the fire. "Think I could use some of that when it's ready," he said.

"Why I made it," Rance said.

B.W. nodded, blinked his eyes several times. "Sorry, I drank too much last night," he said.

"You should be," Rance said, "bad timing. Wait until you're in one of those places you shouldn't be. Next time we might need you."

"Thought you was lookin' at me a little cockeyed," B.W. said. "We're not in the army anymore. I'll do as I damn well please."

"Then find you another partner," Rance said.

"Didn't know we were partners," B.W. said. "Thought we just wound up ridin' together by accident."

"If that's the way you see it, me and the boy will move on," Rance said.

"What makes you think he wants to go with you?" B.W. said.

"Ask him."

"You think you're going to get any of this money you're not," B.W. said. and grabbed the money bags off the ground.

"I don't want it anyway, belongs to other people."

"Good, you'd probably give it to a church or something anyway," B.W. said.

Tommy came walking up with his hat in his hand. "What are you two arguin' about? You woke me up."

"We just realized we don't like each other," B.W. said.

"Why," Tommy said.

"Mr. Holier-Than-Thou here thinks I drink too much," B.W. said.

"Well, you do," Tommy said.

"I guess that's what he told you," B.W. said.

"No. The major said his pa drank too much. You shouldn't get so mad. We need you to be sober to survive."

"The kid's right," Rance said. "You said it yourself, it's dog-eat-dog now."

"I need you both," Tommy said.

B.W. and Rance looked at each other. They knew he was right. They stood there not knowing what to do next, looking off into the wild blue yonder, gathering their thoughts.

Rance was the first to speak. "I been wrong, too, could have got us killed by trying to return that money. Was talkin' out of turn."

"You were, but you're right," B.W. said. "I do drink too much and I know it. Can't seem to know when to quit till after it's too late."

"And I got a mouth problem. Still trying to be a major."

"Why don't you two knock it off and I'll put some flapjacks on," Tommy said.

"Yeah, think I'd like that," B.W. said. "Not as good as biscuits but pretty good if you get 'em done."

"Did you mean what you said, B.W.?" Rance said.

"'Bout what?"

"Not bein' partners."

"No, got my own mouth problems," B.W. said. "Was just mad."

"You want those flapjacks?" Tommy asked.

B.W. and Rance nodded yes.

Tommy fixed the flapjacks. Rance poured himself and B.W. a cup of coffee, handed Tommy his canteen and they ate in silence, then saddled up. B.W. tied the money on his horse and they rode on, letting their horses mosey along at their own speed, stopping to nibble on the grass from time to time. It was high noon before anyone said anything.

"You two still mad?" Tommy said.

B.W. and Rance didn't say anything but shook their head no.

A little further down the trail they came to a sign that read: Texarkana two miles.

"Long way to come to do something useful," B.W. said.

"Only thing we have," Rance said.

"You make a good point, partner," B.W. said, looking at Rance.

Rance smiled. He got the message. "Maybe a cattle train in Texarkana we can catch to Traversville. Could be there tomorrow or the next day."

"I come to like this horse, want to keep him. Named him Dusty," Tommy said.

"Right good name," Rance said.

"Your horse got a name, B.W.?" Tommy asked.

"Yeah...Horse."

19

Back in Milberg, the soldiers that usually came in for dinner every evening at the eatery quit showing up and the local trade had dropped off considerably, something was going on but Julie didn't know what until Colonel Hatch came in a few days later. He stopped inside the door at attention like his knees wouldn't bend, took off his hat and placed a hand on the handle of his sword.

"What can I do for you, colonel?" Julie said.

"Miss Julie, the soldiers won't be coming in anymore. I have posted a bulletin at the fort making your place off limits and strongly suggested to the townspeople that they abstain from patronizing your establishment, as well. The government has determined you're a scarlet woman and a southern sympathizer helping the enemy and a bad influence on the local people."

"That's insane," she said. "You long-winded bastard."

"You just demonstrated why I put out the order," Colonel Hatch said. "Our former marshal believed you knew about Major Allison's jail break and helped plan it. The major and that Indian are combatants working for an underground Confederate organization to start another war and you're a part of it."

"I've never heard such garbage in all my life," Julie said.

"I don't have proof but I think he's right."

"This is my home," Julie said. "I was raised here. All I'm doin' is tryin' to make a livin' and my private life is my own business."

"Might be better all-around if you find another town," Hatch said. "As the magistrate under marshal law, I could close you down for good. I would suggest you sell the place before you go broke."

"I see, and I bet you know someone that would just happen to buy it."

"I do. A mister Walter Peabody has expressed interest in it and will give you a fair price."

"What's your cut, colonel?"

"I hope you don't mean that, Miss Julie. I could have you arrested for those kinds of comments."

"With people like you in charge, colonel, it's going to take forever for this county to come back together."

"I'll send Mr. Peabody by to talk to you tomorrow. Best you take his offer."

"Colonel, most of the people around here have known me all my life. I don't think they will let you get away with running me out of town."

"I would think different with that bastard baby," Hatch said.

"You are a scoundrel," she said. "But I'll do it on one condition."

"What's that?" he said.

"You drop all the charges against Rance Allison, B.W. and the boy. I'll take Mr. Peabody's offer and leave."

"I could take you to jail for threatening me."

"I'm not threatening you, colonel, I'm giving you facts. I can stir up a hornets nest for you with the people in this town if I have a mind to, more trouble than you can imagine."

He stared at her, wiggled his sword handle, took off his hat and wiped his brow. "For the sake of order I'll do it," he said, "If you sell to Mr. Peabody tomorrow, don't discuss any of the details with anyone, and be gone in the next seventy-two hours, I'll drop the charges."

"No posters, no telegrams to any one. Taken off the books," she said.

"Yes."

"You give me your word?"

"Yes. I agree," he said.

"Then we have a deal. If your word is good. If it's not, I'll be back with some help."

"Good evening, ma'am," he said and walked out.

The swinging doors to the kitchen came open and Fannie walked out. "I was listenin' behind the door," she said. "What you goin' to do?"

"What I said I'd do," Julie said. "We got to leave now, Fannie."

The front door opened and the young woman who got off the stage when Paxton and Charlie left walked inside. "Are you Julie?" she asked.

"Yes. Do you want something to eat?"

"No ma'am, I need to tell you something...in private." she said, looking at Fannie.

"Did someone send you?" Julie asked.

"No, ma'am."

"This is Fannie," Julie said. "You can say what you want to in front of her, I'd tell her anyway."

"Very well," the woman said. "I've only been in town a few days but I hear talk from my clients..."

"Clients?" Julie asked.

"At the saloon."

"Oh, those kind of clients."

"Yes, ma'am. My name is Cindy. I used to work in Whiskey Gulch. The boy with those two men that escaped jail is the son of one of the girls I worked with, Alice Woodson. I was afraid to say anything while I was there but from what I hear, you know the two men Tommy is ridin' with. I know who murdered Tommy's mama."

"Go on," Julie said.

"They said Mr. Allison was a friend of yours. I figured they're goin' to Traversville, where Alice came from, to see Tommy's papa. That's where his mama's killer is, too. His name is Booker Church, an ugly man—long face, reminds me of a salamander, with fancy guns and boots. He paid double for a whole night with me, got drunk and told me what he was in Whiskey Gulch for. Said the boy's papa hired him to kill her so she wouldn't cause him no more trouble. Alice made the mistake of sending a telegram to tell him they were coming home. That's why he sent Church to kill her."

"And you didn't tell anyone?" Julie asked.

"He would have killed me."

"You could have told the sheriff."

"He wouldn't have done nothin' anyway. Nobody cares what happens to whores," Cindy said. "I told Alice and she said she could handle it. She had a gun and would kill him. It didn't work out that way."

"I've got no way of getting in touch with Rance now," Julie said.

"When Tommy's papa finds out he's in Traversville, he'll have him and your friend murdered like the boy's mama," Cindy said. "Alice didn't deserve what happened to her. By the way, I was in the saloon the night the Indian killed Allen Dobbs. It was self-defense."

"Can I get you something to drink?" Julie said.

"No ma'am, better get back 'fore they miss me. Don't say I told you anything, Church might still have some friends here."

"I won't," Julie said.

Cindy nodded, picked up the hem of her long purple dress, opened the door and walked out.

"I believe her, Fannie," Julie said. "We'll go to Texas. Rance needs to know about Church and his son. Should have told him when he was here. We spent one night together to comfort each other and I got pregnant. I've always loved him. I'll make a deal with Colonel Hatch's Mr. Peabody tomorrow. If you don't want to go, I'm pretty sure he would let you stay on to run the kitchen for him. I'll leave you some money."

"That's a long way to take a three year old, and we may not get there in time to do any good anyway," Fannie said.

"Already made the deal," Julie said.

"How you plan on gettin' there?" Fannie asked.

"Take a stage out of here and find a train station along the way. You comin?'"

"You're a scarlet woman, Miss Julie. The colonel said so. I don't know if a respectable colored girl like myself should be seen with the likes of you, but I guess I'll take that chance."

Julie smiled. "Let's go check on Mitchell." They put their arms around each other's waists and walked back into the kitchen.

20

Shirley disappeared when the stage got to Pinefield and Preston and Charlie caught the Rebel Express to Texas with an assortment of passengers that included soldiers, cowboys, fancy dans, women and children. There were curtains on the windows and a red flowered design on the carpeted floor with two rows of black leather two-passenger seats that ran the length of the car. Preston had his hat pulled down over his eyes, dozing, and Charlie sat motionless staring out the window as the train rolled along.

A woman and two small boys with their Sunday clothes on were sitting in the seat in front of them. The boys turned around in the seat and stared at Preston and Charlie.

"What's your name?" one of the boys said, looking at Charlie.

Charlie didn't answer and continued looking out the window.

The boy reached over the seat and tapped Charlie on the shoulder. "What's your name," he said, in a louder voice.

"Turn around and leave me alone," Charlie said.

Preston came out from under his hat and put a cold stare on the boys.

Their eyes got big, they gulped and turned around. Preston laid his hat back over his eyes.

"Wonder where that damn woman went," Charlie said.

Preston raised his hat and looked at Charlie. "Everyone knew what she would do, except you."

"She borrowed fifty dollars from me," Charlie said. "Lot of money for nothing."

"She didn't borrow it, she stole it."

"Can't believe I was that stupid."

"I can," Preston said. "A woman has a way of confusing a man when he's thinkin' 'bout dippin' his wick."

Charlie tightened his lips and shook his head. "That's damn sure right."

The woman with the boys stuck her head around the side of her seat so she could see Preston and Charlie. "I forbid you to use that kind of language in the presence of my children."

"You wouldn't have heard us if you wasn't eavesdropping," Preston said. "Mind your own damn business."

"Well I never..." she said.

"Looks like you have," Preston said, "You got two kids, you just don't remember how."

"You're a very unpleasant man," she said to Preston, jerked her head back toward the front of the car, grabbing the boys and pushing them down in the seat. "Shut up and sit still 'fore I tan your hides."

The conductor entered the car. He was stoop-shouldered with a gray handlebar mustache. He kind of shuffled when he walked, like he had something wrong with his hip or leg. He stopped about halfway down the car and looked around.

"Listen up, folks," he said. "Going to spend the night in Buffalo Flats and pick up soldiers and mail. You can find you a place to bed down and the railroad will pay for it. We leave at seven-thirty sharp in the mornin' and anyone not here is on their own."

"Think I'll stay on the train," Charlie said.

"So you got snookered again ," Preston said. "Won't be the last time and we got a long way to go, might better get a bed while you can, since the railroads goin' to pay."

"Yeah guess so," Charlie said.

When they pulled into Buffalo Flats everyone got off the train and made their way downtown.

Preston and Charlie stopped in front of the Fast Hitch Saloon. A sign in the window read: Beds fifty cents a night, furnished three dollars.

"This should do," Preston said and they walked in with several other men to the bar and sat their bags down. They glanced at two painted-up young whores leaning against the bar, smiling at them.

The bartender wiped his hands on his apron. "What'll it be, gents?"

"Two whiskeys," Preston said and laid a silver dollar on the bar.

The bartender sat two glasses on the bar, poured the whiskey and picked up the silver dollar.

"Need two beds," Preston said.

"You want that furnished?" he said.

"Not tonight," Preston said. Charlie nodded in agreement.

"Okay," the bartender said. "Without the whores that's a dollar."

Preston and Charlie handed him the money and he gave Preston a key. "Two beds, room four, top of the stairs. Your bags will be waitin' for you."

"Thanks," Preston said.

They picked up their glasses and turned around. The saloon was almost full with train passengers and locals. A slightly plump whore with a bright red dress and hair to match was sitting in the lap of a cowboy playing Faro.

Preston walked over to a nearby table where three men were playing poker and Charlie followed.

"Man, get a hand in this game," Preston said.

One of the men looked up at Preston. It was Billy Shaw. He had on his sheriff's badge and was packing his ivory-handled Colt. "You come in on the train?" Billy said

"Sure did," Preston said.

"No IOUs, money up front to cover your bets," Billy said.

"Good enough," Preston said and sat down.

A burly-looking cuss wearing overalls with a dirty beard pitched his cards out on the table and poured himself a glass of whiskey. The other one did the same and leaned back in his chair and looked at Preston like he was sizing him up. He was lean, narrow-jawed and solemn looking. He had on a stove top hat, black coat vest and pants.

"What 'bout you," Billy said to Charlie.

"I'll just watch if that's okay?" Charlie said.

"As long as you sit behind your partner where his cards are the only ones you see," Billy said.

Charlie nodded and sat down behind Preston, drank the rest of the whiskey and sat the empty glass on the table.

"This here is Ned Martin," Billy said and pointed at the dirty bearded guy, "and this is the undertaker, Crawford Smart." Both men nodded.

"Willie Preston."

"Name sounds familiar," Billy said. "Weren't you a marshal from over Kansas way?"

"Was a time back, been marshaling in Milberg, Virginia until recently," Preston said. "Bounty huntin' now."

"Who you lookin' for?" Billy said.

"An Indian, a one-armed man and a boy, killed a man in Whiskey Gulch and maybe three more. You seen 'em?"

"They been here," Ned said, "don't forget somebody like that. Was here when they rode in with the two Bannister boys layin' across their saddles."

"That right, sheriff?" Preston said.

"They said the boys came flying out of the woods, shootin' at 'em," Billy said. "Didn't have a choice but to kill 'em. Couldn't prove otherwise, had to let 'em go. Didn't know about the other trouble, though."

"We goin' to gossip or play cards," Ned said and took a big swig of whiskey straight from the bottle.

"Play cards." Billy picked up the deck, shuffled the cards and dealt everyone a hand.

They were still playing at two in the morning. Ned went broke and called it a night but Crawford and Billy were trying to get back what they lost to Preston.

"Think I'll turn in," Charlie said.

"Shouldn't take long to get the rest of their money," Preston said and smiled. Crawford and Billy found no humor in it.

"Tell you what," Billy said. "One hand for what I got left."

"I'll go for that," Crawford said.

"Okay," Preston said. "I'll match what each of you has. Five card stud, face up, no draw, best hand wins."

They both nodded.

Charlie sat back down. "I gotta see this."

Preston dealt the hands. Crawford had high card, no pairs. Billy had two jacks and Preston two kings.

"Looks like you're out of money, boys," Preston said and drug the money across the table to his side. "Buy you a drink 'fore you go?"

"Not me," Crawford said and stood up. "Got two stiffs to bury in the morning. Have to charge more now to cover my losses." He repositioned his stove top hat on his head and walked out of the saloon.

Billy sat there. "I'll take that drink," he said. Preston picked up the whiskey bottle and poured Billy a full glass of whiskey.

"There you go, drink up," Preston said.

"Thanks, wanted a bit of conversation with you in private anyway," Billy said and looked around the saloon. No one close enough to hear him except Preston and Charlie.

"What you got on your mind, sheriff?" Preston said.

"Bout them men you chasin' after. You need any help?"

"Nope," Preston said, filling his pockets with Billy and Crawford's money.

"You know where they're goin' at least?" Billy asked.

"I do," Preston said.

"You include me," Billy said, "and I can tell you something that'll make it worth your while."

"Might consider it," Preston said.

"Need your word 'fore I tell you."

"What you get out of it? No reward for them, got a personal reason?"

"You'll know when I tell you."

"Okay, better be good then," Preston said.

"I got your word?"

"You have. What is it?"

"Them three you're after killed two boys that robbed a bank in Pinefield," Billy said. "They got the money. They brought the dead boys in sayin' they was the ones robbed the bank. Had over seven-thousand dollars of the bank's money still in the sacks on the Bannister Boys' horses. Said they was taking it back to the bank. I knew they wasn't goin to do that so I tried to arrest them but they bushwhacked me and left me out on the trail. I barely did make it back alive. They still got the money."

"Why didn't they kill you?" Preston said. "I would have."

"Don't know. I came back here like nothing ever happened. I'm the only one knows 'bout the money. Thought maybe we could partner up. Kill 'em, split the money. No one would ever know the real story 'cept us."

"Now that I know about the money, why would I want to include you?" Preston said.

"You gave your word. I got a badge to make you my deputies. We'll be the law, everything nice and legal. I'll show you one of the Pinefield Bank bags in the morning to prove my story."

"Pretty convincin,'" Preston said.

"We got a deal then?"

"We do."

"Meet you in the morning," Billy said. "Seven-thirty at the train station."

Preston nodded and Billy stuck out his hand and Preston shook hands with him.

"Let's get some sleep, Charlie," Preston said and they headed up the stairs, Billy watching.

Preston and Charlie went to their room. Charlie struck a match to light the lamp and Preston blew it out and walked over to the window and looked out. Billy was crossing the street to his horse tied to a hitching post in front of the sheriff's office.

"Stay here, Charlie." Preston took his hat off and handed it to Charlie, opened the window and climbed out, laid down on the roof, slid down to the edge and dropped down to the ground. Two riders riding away from him were the only ones on the street. He crossed the street and walked up behind Billy, drew his Arkansas toothpick and held it beside his leg.

"Billy," he said and Billy turned around.

Billy looked at Preston and saw the knife, but wasn't quick enough to draw his Colt before Preston plunged the knife into his throat and ripped his jugular out. Billy staggered against his horse. The horse pulled on the reins tied to the hitching post and Billy fell face down on the ground without so much as a grunt, his ivory-handled Colt halfway out of his holster, his blood spilling out on the ground.

Preston looked down at Billy's crumpled body. "You're kind of stupid, Billy boy." He put the knife back in his boot, dropped Billy's Colt back in the holster and lifted him on his horse and tied him across the saddle with Billy's lariat, slapped the horse on the butt hard and it took off for parts unknown.

Preston scattered dirt over the blood with his boots in the moonlight and hurried back across the street without seeing anyone. He swung up on the roof and crawled back in the room, Charlie watching it all from the window.

"Takes care of that," Preston said. "Now we're the only ones that knows besides those three we're after. Got seven-thousand more reasons to find them now."

"Didn't figure you was goin' to let him come with us," Charlie said. "Hope you're not goin to do that to me."

"Nope, I need you," Preston said.

"How was you sure he was tellin' the truth?"

"He wouldn't have offered to show us the bank bag if he wasn't."

Preston pulled off his boots and wiped the blood off the knife and his boots with a towel and stuck the towel in his bag, the knife back in his boot, and laid down on the bed, waiting for the next day to catch another train.

21

When Rance, B.W. and Tommy rode into Texarkana, they started looking for a livery stable to feed the horses. Tommy saw the mercantile store and kept riding to get some peppermint sticks. Rance and B.W. rode into the livery and dismounted. Rance noticed Tommy wasn't there.

"Where'd that boy go?" Rance asked.

"Was behind us coming in," B.W. said.

They remounted and turned their horses around and rode back out in the street. No sign of Tommy.

They rode all over town but didn't find Tommy and so they headed back to the livery stable. When they stopped at the door, Tommy came riding in behind them.

"Where you been?" B.W. said. "Scared the hell out of us."

"I can take care of myself.," he said. "Got me some peppermints, heard the train whistle blow and went to the train station."

"Why'd you do that," B.W. said. "Don't wander off like that again. Don't you know who's following us?"

"Well, what did you find out?" Rance said.

"The next train outta here leaves at four this afternoon, pullin' passenger and cattle cars. We can put our horses in a cattle car, ride in a passenger car all the way to Traversville. I told the ticket agent you was my uncles and sent me to buy the tickets."

"Where'd you get the money," Rance said.

"Took three ten-dollar gold pieces out of the bag the other day in case I needed money."

"Well, it's alright," B.W. said, "but that's stealing."

"What you think you're doing," Tommy said, looking at B.W.

"That's different," B.W. said.

"Not really," Rance said, "just more money."

"Are you going to preach to me again?" B.W. said.

"It's his money too," Rance said.

"It is," B.W. said. "Just don't think he should take it without telling us."

"You two hush. We got a train to catch." Tommy said.

"He's right, kinda silly us arguing over nothin.' Lead the way, Mr. Travers," Rance said.

"I want to stop at the store and get me some more peppermint sticks," Tommy said. "Long ride ahead."

"Whatever you say," B.W. said.

Tommy got his peppermint sticks and they rode on to the train station. Several men were coming and going on and off the train.

"That the guy you talked to?" Rance said, looking at a big-headed man with a railroad cap on that looked like it was having trouble staying on his fat head. He was wearing the Travers overalls but had the side buttons lose to accommodate a bulging belly.

"Yeah that's him," Tommy said.

"Since you're the one that was talking to him," Rance said, "ask him where he wants the horses."

Tommy handed Rance the reins to his horse. The agent saw Tommy walking toward him.

"Hello young man. Those your uncles?" he said, looking at Rance and B.W.

"Yes sir," he said. "They want to know where to put the horses."

"Uncles," B.W. said, looking at Rance, both smiling.

"Didn't know one of them was an Indian," he said, eyeing B.W. "Might not should let him on board. You got Indian blood? Might not let you either."

"Not really my uncle, I just call him that. He pretty well stays to himself, won't bother nobody," Tommy said.

"Make sure he stays away from the other passengers," the man said.

"Yes sir, I will."

"Tell them to put the horses in the first cattle car. After that, get your tickets and get aboard, only bout an hour before we leave. Don't know if they will feed the Indian when we stop in Winfield."

Tommy nodded and walked back to Rance and B.W.

"We heard," B.W. said. "You sure I'm good enough to ride with the white folks?"

"Had to keep him from takin' our tickets away," Tommy said. "Might have to ride them horses the rest of the way on my sore butt."

"We don't have to get on the train if you don't want to, B.W.," Rance said.

"I'll manage," B.W. said. "Let's get the horses loaded." B.W. took the money bags off his horse.

They led the horses on the car, grabbed the Henrys and the shotgun and unsaddled the horses, closed the gate and walked up to the passenger car.

The ticket agent came running up to them. "That Indian can't get on board with them guns and that tomahawk," he said. "He got a gun in them saddle bags?"

"No, personal things," Rance said.

B.W. handed his guns to Rance. Rance handed them to the train man.

"What about the tomahawk," the agent said.

B.W. pulled the tomahawk out of his belt and handed it to the railroad man and glance down at his boot with the knife in it, picked up the money bags and started walking down the aisle of the car.

People placed bags in their seats and sat kids in them to keep him from sitting down. He walked all the way to the back of the car and sat down by himself and placed the suitcase beside him.

"What's he doin' that for?" Tommy asked.

"Let him be. He's doin' it for you," Rance said.

"For me?" Tommy said.

"You'll know soon enough, go on back," Rance said, pointing at the back of the car. They sat down next to B.W. The nearest passenger was four rows in front of them.

"May need another war," B.W. said.

"Might have to be on your side next time," Rance said.

"How much one of them Gatling's cost?" B.W. said, placed his hand on the suitcase and tapped it with his fingers.

"Know what you're thinking," Rance said, "but this train may belong to Tommy."

"Ya'll talkin' in riddles," Tommy said.

"That we are," B.W. said. "No need for you to know."

A short, dumpy little man with a gray beard and a big gut stood up and looked at B.W. "Aint ridin' no train with a stinkin' Injun. Might as well be a nigger." He grabbed his suitcase and headed for the door.

B.W. rose up in his seat and Rance put a hand on his shoulder. "We're gettin' off," Rance said.

B.W. eased back down in his seat. "No, we need to get to Traversville. I'll stay here and try not to kill anyone for now."

They heard a whistle and the train began to roll away from the depot, smoke running past the windows as the train picked up speed. Seconds later, the train was at full speed headed for Traversville.

Four hours later, when the train pulled into the Traversville depot, they followed the other passengers off the train. The conductor gave them their weapons and they headed for the cattle car to get their horses when they heard a woman's voice behind them.

"Mister Indian," the voice said and they turned around. There stood a little old white lady wearing a flowered cotton dress and a bonnet, holding her parasol over her head in the Texas heat. She took a step closer to B.W. "Mister Indian," she said, "wanted you to know I didn't mind riding with you, even if you are an Indian."

B.W. took off his hat. "Thank you, ma'am," he said. She nodded, turned and toddled off.

Rance grinned at B.W. "You know," Rance said. "I don't mind ridin' with you either, even though you're not a complete Indian."

"She meant well. Nobody knows but you." B.W. said. "Let's get the horses."

They got their horses and saddled them, B.W. holding on to the money bags as they rode down the street looking at the town. Pretty much like all the rest they passed through along the way, he thought. They rode by a bank and B.W. took a long look at it.

"Why you lookin' at that bank?" Rance said. "You're makin' me nervous."

"Was thinkin' 'bout our money. A safe place to put it," B.W. said. "Need to buy that ranch 'fore something happens to it."

"Still havin' some problems with that. Should do somethin' useful with it," Rance said.

"I am," B.W. said, "goin' to buy us a ranch."

"Don't know if I want a ranch, need two good hands for that," Rance said.

"I'll be your other hand," B.W. said.

"Can't turn something like that down," Rance said.

"I want to find my mama's killer," Tommy said.

"Kind of think that would be my priority too," B.W. said.

"Your what?" Tommy said.

"The thing I would want to do first."

Tommy nodded.

"Let's find us a place to bed down and get a bath and some clean clothes," Rance said. "Then think on the rest."

"There he goes with that bath thing again, B.W.," Tommy said.

"Maybe we do need a bath," B.W. said.

"I don't believe my ears," Rance said. "You mean you don't think you smell like tree bark anymore?"

"Don't get too carried away. It'll be a quick one."

"Cleanliness is next to godliness," Rance said and grinned.

"Man, are you full of shit," B.W. said.

Rance smiled.

They crossed over to the next street and saw Ferguson Bed and Bath Boarding House on a sign out front.

"That looks good," Rance said. "Want to try it?"

"Might as well," B.W. said.

"Guess I'll go too," Tommy said.

They tied their horses to the hitching post and dismounted, B.W. holding on to the money bags. They walked up to the door and rang the bell.

A young woman appeared and opened the door. She had long blonde hair with a pink ribbon in it, big blue eyes, wearing a long blue dress holding a white cat. "He'll run out the door if I put him down," she said. "Come on in." They walked in and closed the door. She shifted the cat to hold him with both hands and sat him down and he ran off.

"I'm the owner, Rhonda Jennings," she said. "You need a bed?"

"Yes ma'am," Rance said.

"Can give you and the boy a room, the Indian will have to sleep on the back porch, bathe in the creek."

"No ma'am, I won't do that," B.W. said.

"Then go somewhere else. This is my place and I make the rules. You're no different than a nigger around here. The other guests would leave."

"I am what I am, ma'am, don't have no apologies to make," B.W. said.

"Neither do I," she said.

"Good day ma'am." Rance opened the door and they walked back outside and she closed the door.

"Even the cat's white," B.W. said as they walked away.

"Well look at it this way," Rance said. "You won't have to sleep in a bed after all and a creek is warm this time of year."

"Why don't you and Tommy stay there and I'll find a place, would feel better 'bout it that way."

"No way, partner, it's all or none."

"Goes for me too," Tommy said.

"Let's find the livery stable," Rance said. "Bet they got a hay loft. Beginnin' to feel at home in one."

They turned their horses around and rode past the sheriff's office.

"Wonder if they got a wanted poster on us here?" Rance said.

"We'll find out soon enough," B.W. said. "Think that marshal is still comin?'"

"Been over a month since we high-tailed it out of Milberg, but could be," Rance said as they rode up to the livery stable.

Two boys younger than Tommy were playing in front of the livery and a man inside the open doors with no shirt on was filing a horse's hoof. He was tall and muscled with a head full of blonde hair and had an eye patch over his right eye. Rance's horse snorted and the man looked up, dropped the horse's leg and walked up to the door. "Need to bed those horses down?" he asked.

"Us too," Rance said. "The boardin' house don't think too highly of Indians."

"Not many people round here do," he said. "Name's Riley Jones. Don't have a problem myself, spent some time with the Cherokees 'fore the war."

B.W. smiled. "That's me," he said.

"Looks like you was in the war too," Rance said.

"Was in the last battle of the war two weeks after Lee surrendered to Grant. Neither side knew the war was over, Battle of Palmetto Ranch. We won the battle but lost the war. Had two good eyes till a cannon ball busted too close to me 'fore it was over. Anyways...fifty cents a day for each of the horses. You can unsaddle and put 'em in a stall, I'll give 'em grain, hay and water after I finish shoein' this horse. No charge to sleep in the hay loft, just don't leave here with anythin' you didn't come in with."

"Fair enough," B.W. said.

"Where can we all get a bath?" Rance asked.

"Big Sally's Saloon just down the street, long as you got the money."

"That include Indians?" B.W. said.

"Don't matter what you are, Big Sally's only got one rule. You better pay what you owe or one of the girls will cut your balls off. Oh, sorry bout that, son," he said, looking at Tommy.

"Could we get you to hang on to our personals while we take care of ourselves?" Rance said.

"You can," Riley said.

They unsaddled their horses and handed Riley the rifles, shotgun and saddle bags. Rance kept his Colt and B.W. his and the tomahawk. B.W. picked up the money bags.

"I can watch that too, if you like," Riley said.

"Think I'll hold on to it," B.W. said.

Riley nodded and they walked out into the street.

The Big Sally Saloon had large painted pictures of skimpily-dressed women on the windows on both sides of the swinging doors. A cowpoke came flying out the swinging doors and rolled into the street. A man big as a Texas mountain with a thick black mustache, garters on his arms and an apron tied around his huge waist came through the swinging doors. He had curly black hair and dark brown eyes. He was a head taller than B.W. and a hundred pounds heavier. He tossed a hat and a gun into the street and pointed a big long finger at the cowboy. "You ever come back in here I'll cut you up for dog meat. Nobody makes fun of me," he said and walked back into the saloon.

The cowboy grabbed his hat and gun, scrambled to his feet and ran down the street as fast as he could.

The mountain of a man was standing behind the bar when they walked in. A big long mirror on the wall behind him revealed the back of his huge bear-like shoulders and arms.

Yankees and rebel soldiers in uniform, cowboys and sod busters were standing side by side at the bar, belting whiskey down.

"What'll you have?" the man asked.

"Whiskey," B.W. said and sat the bags down and placed his boot on them.

The big man placed two glasses on the bar and poured the whiskey. "Got some sarsaparilla for your boy if he wants it."

Rance looked at Tommy, he nodded yes and the bartender poured the sarsaparilla.

"You may not know, but the federals moved in in June and took over," the big man said. "Have to check your guns or they'll take you in. So if you will hand them over and that tomahawk until you leave we can get on with things."

They handed the mountain the guns and the tomahawk and he set them behind the bar.

"First one is on the house, fifty cents a shot after that," he said and poured them another drink and held out his hand. B.W. fished a five-dollar gold coin out of his pocket and laid it in his hand. "Keep it," B.W. said. "Not through."

He held the gold piece up and stuck it in his mouth to test it. "If you want to come back later without the boy I can find you some good female company."

"Need a bath and some fresh clothes right now," Rance said.

"Name's Big Sally," he said. "Should know don't take kindly to anybody makin' fun of my name."

"We saw that," B.W. said.

Big Sally nodded. "Have to pay the girls extra if you want them with you in the bath," he said. "The boy will have to bathe later if you do."

"Just the bath. I'm trying to quit," B.W. said and pushed his empty glass toward Big Sally for a refill and Rance smiled.

Big Sally smiled and poured the whiskey. "Like a man with a sense of humor," he said. "Hot baths are three dollars, in advance."

"We'll take it," Rance said. "Pay him, B.W. Give him a ten-dollar gold piece and let him keep the change." Tommy made a horrible face and shook his head no. B.W. tossed the gold piece on the bar.

"Think I'm goin' to like you boys," Big Sally said.

B.W. and Tommy looked at Rance then each other and shrugged.

"Have a seat and I'll bring you a bottle while you wait on the water to heat. Café next door when you get hungry."

Rance and B.W. nodded. B.W. picked up the money, they took their glasses with them and walked over to a table and sat down. "Kind of free with our money there, partner," B.W. said.

"Setting up an information source," Rance said. B.W. tilted his head slightly and started nudging the money bags with his foot. "Bullshit."

Big Sally brought a bottle of whiskey and the sarsaparilla bottle over and sat them on the table. Two whores started over to the table and Big Sally waved them off.

"When we goin' to see my pa?" Tommy said.

"Don't know yet," B.W. said. He picked up the whiskey bottle and poured himself another drink.

Tommy and Rance watched as B.W. poured the glass full.

"Might better slow down on the whiskey, B.W.," Rance said.

B.W. nodded, drank the glass of whiskey and turned the glass upside down.

A dapper-looking man walked in dressed in a well-fitting cream-colored suit wearing a white Stetson, shiny black boots and stepped up to the bar.

Big Sally nodded to him. "The usual, Mister Travers?" The name got their attention. He didn't look much different than he did in the picture.

"Give me a double, Sally," he said. "Been a hard day dealin' with all them damn Yankees tryin' to tell me how to run my railroad."

"Got some new brandy in, supposed to be the best," Sally said.

Travers nodded and slid his glass toward Sally and he poured it full. "On the house, Mr. Travers, you spend enough with me to get a free drink once in a while."

"That's right neighborly of you," Travers said, made a saluting motion to Sally with the glass and downed the brandy.

"Smooth," he said. "Got to go, Maggie's waitin.'" He turned away from the bar and saw Tommy. "You think it's a good idea to let children in here, Sally?"

"Just passin' through," Big Sally said. "Came in for a bath, waitin' for the water to heat. Be leavin' after that."

Travers walked over to their table. "Where you boys from?"

"A little of everywhere," Rance said.

"Lookin' for a job?"

"Nope, come to see you, just didn't know it would be this soon," Rance said.

"Me? Do I know you?"

"No, but you will," B.W. said. "Best we talk in private, though."

"You from the government?"

"No, more of a personal matter," B.W. said.

"Like what?"

"Not now," Rance said.

"Don't play games with me, boy," Travers said. "I don't like it. If you got somethin' stuck in your craw then spit it out."

"We will at the right time," Rance said.

"Stay away from me," Travers said and stormed out of the saloon.

"Now look what you done," Sally said. "You insulted my best customer and benefactor. Weren't for him I wouldn't have this place. He kept them damn Yankees from closing me down. He was just tryin' to be friendly."

"We're not, let him be friendly with someone else," B.W. said.

"What you got against Mr. Travers?" Big Sally said.

"I want to go now," Tommy said, tears in his eyes.

"Think we'll pass on the bath," Rance said.

"You don't get a refund." Sally said.

"That's okay, we're leavin' now," Rance said.

They stood up. B.W. picked up the money bags and they walked outside.

"You think Travers figured out who Tommy is," Rance said.

"Could be," B.W. said.

"I don't want you to go see him," Tommy said. "I don't want him to know."

"We've come a long way for nothing if we don't," B.W. said.

"It was you two that was so all fired up," Tommy said. "I told you before I don't care about it. You just want to be big shots. Leave him alone."

"I guess we weren't listenin,'" Rance said. "The only thing we wanted was for you to have what was rightfully yours."

"We both thought we were doin' the right thing," B.W. said. "Never thought you had any feelin's for him after what he did."

"I don't. He can have his damn railroad. I'm goin' to the livery stable."

"Don't you think you should eat?" Rance said.

"Not that hungry anymore," he said and walked away.

They waited for Tommy to be out of earshot. "Looks like we got to do some thinkin' about this. Guess it was quite a shock for him to see his pa like that for the first time," Rance said.

"Yeah, we're askin' him to handle somethin' most grown men couldn't," B.W. said.

"Was goin' to get somethin' to eat but I kinda lost my appetite."

"Yeah me too. Even biscuits and whiskey don't sound good right now."

Rance made a face and shook his head. "Best we leave the boy alone for a while. What you goin' to do with them saddle bags? You can't keep waggin' 'em around."

"I ain't lettin' this money out of my sight until we spend it or find a safe place for it."

"Let's go back to the livery and see what Tommy's up to," Rance said.

B.W. nodded and they headed for the livery stable.

About a hour later, a tall skinny man wearing a sheriff's badge came in the livery carrying a double-barrel shotgun. Riley was sitting at a small table drinking coffee, Tommy chewing a peppermint stick, Rance drinking coffee and B.W. sipping whiskey with the money bags sitting beside his foot. The shotgun and the rifles were on the table.

"Why are you botherin' Mister Travers?" the sheriff said.

"Personal business," Rance said.

"I'm Sheriff Seaton Odom. Answer my question 'fore I get nervous and blow a hole in you."

B.W. shoved the money bag under the table with his foot under a stack of old harnesses.

"Like I said, it's personal," Rance said.

"He's my papa," Tommy said.

B.W. and Rance looked at Tommy. "Thought you weren't goin' to do that," Rance said.

"Changed my mind. You're right, part of that damn railroad is mine."

"What're you tryin' to pull?" Sheriff Odom said.

"I'm his son," Tommy said. "My name's Thomas Travers."

"No way," Odom said.

"It's the truth," Rance said. "That's why we wanted to talk to him in private."

"I don't know what you jackrabbits are up to, but you're goin' to jail until I do." Sheriff Odom raised his shotgun toward them. "Don't go for them guns or I'll blow you to kingdom come. Get on your feet and get out of here. I'll be right behind you."

"Riley," Rance said, "go tell Travers what's goin' on and tell him he needs to talk to us about Alice and his son. Would you do that?"

"I can," Riley said.

"Thanks," Rance said.

"Riley Jones, this ain't none of your business," Odom said. "Now you three head out that door, you're goin' to jail."

"The boy too?" B.W. asked.

"Yeah, the boy too."

They walked out the livery stable door and across the street to the jail, the sheriff holding the shotgun on them. They went inside and he directed them to a jail cell with a bar window, two iron cots with soiled mattresses and a piss bucket. He picked up the cell keys and opened the door. "Get in there."

They went in the cell and he locked it behind them.

"This place stinks," Tommy said.

"Ain't no hotel," Odom said and eased the hammers down on the shotgun. "Gonna go see what Mister Travers wants to do with you." He walked out of the jail and closed the door.

"Everybody keeps puttin' us in jail." B.W. sat down on a cot and Rance and Tommy sat down on the other one.

About an hour later, Travers and the sheriff came in. Travers walked up up to the cell door, looking at Tommy.

"You're saying that's my boy?"

"It is," Rance said.

"The woman and the boy were killed in Virginia during the war," Travers said. "Got a letter from my cousin sayin' so."

"Murdered would be more like it," Rance said. "Somehow the boy survived."

"I'm a lawyer," B.W. said. "We're goin' to take you to court for his share of the railroad."

"Well first," Travers said, "I don't believe you're a lawyer. Second, ain't a judge in these parts goin' against me. He knows what would happen to him."

"If it wasn't for my mama you could go to hell," Tommy said. "But I'm doin' this for her, you sonofabitch."

"No son of mine would ever talk that way to me," Travers said.

"He would if he was raised in a saloon," Rance said.

"I don't believe any of this," Travers said. "But to keep it off the streets and put an end to it, I'll give you a thousand dollars to ride out of here with the boy and never come back."

"You let us out of here first," B.W. said, "and we'll talk."

"No talkin' to no one, that's the deal. I advise you to take it or you can stay in there till you rot."

"Let us out of here and show us the money," B.W. said.

"I'll give you the money tomorrow. Until then you'll stay in jail to show you I mean business," Travers said and walked out.

"You're not really goin' to take that money, are you?" Tommy said.

"No, just wanted out of jail. May just kill him like I wanted to," B.W. said. "I'll think it over tonight."

"No," Rance said, "the boy don't need it bad enough for us to kill him."

22

Willie Preston picked up his shotgun and bag and stepped up on the car, Charlie close behind with his gear. They walked down the aisle, found a seat and sat down. The bushy-haired fat agent came on board and collected everyone's tickets. When he walked up to Preston and Charlie he looked at the double-barrel shotgun leaning against the seat. "Those things always make me nervous," he said, "blow a man in half."

"Just about," Preston said.

The fat man nodded. "Had an Indian try to bring one on board a few days ago, made him get rid of it."

"What'd he look like?"

"A big one, long black hair dressed in black with a feather in his hat. Don't know what tribe, though. Creepy lookin' fella."

"By himself?"

"No, was with a one-armed man and a boy."

"Where was they headed?"

"Traversville, same as you yesterday," he said and walked on down the aisle.

"Well, you were right, marshal," Charlie said.

"Don't call me that anymore, Charlie. We don't want anyone in Traversville to know about me."

"Okay, just got so used to it. Hard habit to break," Charlie said. "How we goin' to kill 'em?"

"Keep your voice down."

Charlie leaned closer to Preston and whispered, "Ain't goin' to be easy, however we do it. They're soldiers, know somethin' about killin.' May be best to shoot 'em in the back."

"I'll do the thinkin', you do the shootin' when I tell you."

"Way it's always been," Charlie said. "We're goin' to need horses, would hate to be stranded there and have to steal one."

"Wouldn't be your first time, would it?" Preston said. "Checked you out 'fore I hired you. Was wanted for horse rustling back in Kansas. Figured it was cause of the war and let it go."

"Was just tryin' to keep them from the rebels," Charlie said.

"Sure you were."

"That's the gospel truth."

"Don't matter now anyway." Preston slid down in the seat and pushed his hat over his eyes.

"You know, marsh...uh, Willie, I ain't ever goin' to trust another woman as long as I live."

Preston raised his hat up. "First time one shakes her tail at you, you won't remember a damn thing."

"Don't think so," Charlie said. "How far is it from Texarkana to Traversville?"

Preston raised his hat up again. "Charlie, I can't get no sleep with you talkin' me to death. I don't know, supposed to be there in the morning. Now shut up and let me get some rest." He placed his hat back over his eyes.

The next morning, Preston and Charlie were the only ones that got off at Traversville and the train moved on to Austin. They picked up their gear and walked across the tracks and saw a livery stable sign at the end of the street.

"Let's get some transportation," Preston said and they walked on down the street to the stable.

Riley Jones was feeding horses when they walked in.

Charlie spotted Rance's buckskin and looked at Preston. Preston nodded.

Riley sat the feed sack down and walked over to them and looked at the bags they were carrying.

"You just get off the train?"

"We did," Preston said.

"Looks like you need some horses."

"We do." Preston sat their gear down and cradled the double-barrel in the crook of his arm as he looked around.

"Where's the boys that owns them horses," Preston said.

"Sheriff come rushin' in here this mornin' and took 'em to jail," Riley said. "Been sleepin' in the loft."

"What he take 'em in for?" Preston asked.

"Said they threatened Mr. Travers. He's a big shot around here, owns the railroad, people kind of cater to him to make sure they stay on his good side."

"That the only reason?"

"Far as I know. Whatever Travers says is pretty much the law."

"How much for two horses with tack?"

"Oh, forty dollars would do it, I guess, for the ones in the corral," Riley said.

"Let's have a look." Preston walked out back to look at the horses. "Not the best lookin' ones I seen but they should do for now." He gave Riley thirty dollars.

"You're ten short," Riley said.

"Nope, that's it," Preston said, "all they're worth."

Riley looked at the money, then looked back at Preston.

"Okay," Riley said. "I'll get 'em saddled for you. Already fed and watered them."

"We'll help, want to take a look around town," Preston said.

"Not a whole lot to look at," Riley said. "Lot of saloons and hungry people, no work. People robbin' their neighbors. Big Sally Saloon's close by if you want a drink or female company."

"Might get that drink, think my pal here has sworn off women, though," Preston said and grinned.

"That a fact?" Riley said.

"Depends on the woman," Charlie said.

They saddled the horses and Preston and Charlie rode out of the livery stable.

"The blacksmith said they been sleepin' in the livery," Preston said. "The money might be in the livery stable since they was whisked away to jail so sudden-like."

"Think the sheriff found it?" Charlie asked.

"Have to check it out."

"What about the smith?"

"More likely he found it if anyone did," Preston said. "If he gets in the way or he's got the money, kill 'em."

"Think I'll take that buckskin, too," Charlie said.

"Fine with me long as we get the money."

"What do we do 'bout them?"

"Let 'em be, don't have to worry 'bout them long as they're in jail," Preston said. "We get that money, ain't gonna be concerned 'bout marshalin' no more no how."

"How come you all-fired sure they got the money? That Johnny Reb may have been lyin'," Charlie said.

"What other reason could he have had for wantin' to go."

"Where we goin' after we get the money?"

"Arizona," Preston said. "Don't have much law out there, man can build an empire with some money if he don't care who he steps on."

"Don't matter to me who they are."

"That's why I let you come along, Charlie, you got no scruples and that's the kind of man I need right now. That changes, though, I might have to kill you."

Charlie laughed. It never occurred to him that Preston meant it.

"I'm feeling better now," Charlie said. "Might buy me a handsome woman."

"We don't have time," Preston said. "After we eat we'll go back to the livery for the money, start with the smith."

"Don't you feed prisoners around here?" B.W. said.

It was ten in the morning and Sheriff Odom had just arrived.

"When I want to. Got your money, goin' to let you out," he said and handed B.W. an envelope through the bars. You got two hours to get out of town or we'll bury you here. Dropped your weapons off at the livery. Don't load them till you're out of town. Now get."

When they walked in the livery stable, they saw Riley lying beside the feed bin.

"Is he dead?" B.W. said and tried to find the money bags under the harnesses. They were gone.

"He' s alive." Rance kneeled down beside him and raised his head. Riley let out a moan and opened his eyes. There was a big bloody gash on his forehead and several cuts on his face.

"What happened?" B.W. said.

"After they took you to jail, two fellas I sold some horses to came back and started pistol-whipping me, askin' about money you had. Tried to tell them I didn't know anythin' about it. They found some saddle bags under the table and tried to steal your horses, too, but they couldn't get a saddle on and left 'em."

"Holy hell, they got our money!" B.W. said.

"Need a doctor?" Rance asked Riley.

"Don't think so."

"Did you hear me," B.W. said, looking at Rance.

"I heard you."

"Hear any names, Riley?" B.W. said.

"One of them called the other one Charlie when he was trying to put a saddle on the buckskin."

"Charlie a big man, kinda barrel-chested?" Rance said.

"Yes," Riley said. "The other one was tall, slim and had a black mustache. An ornery-lookin' cuss totin' a tied-down .44. You know 'em?"

"Yeah, we know 'em. Did you see which way they went?" B.W. said.

"No. They said they came in on the train."

"How did they know we were here?" Tommy said.

"Told you, Preston knows his business," Rance said.

"Why didn't they come get us then," Tommy said.

"Found that money in the saddle bags first. Probably didn't care about us anymore," Rance said.

"There was money in the saddle bags?" Riley asked.

"We got to get it back." B.W. said.

"Let 'em have it," Rance said. "It's tainted money."

"I don't care if it's covered in dog shit, I want it back," B.W. said.

Riley started to get up and grabbed his head and sat back down. "Damn that hurts."

"Major, you take care of Tommy, I'll go get the money," B.W. said.

"The money's not worth getting killed over," Rance said.

"Don't intend to."

"I can't let you go by yourself," Rance said. "Tommy, saddle the horses, fill the canteens and some goat bags of water for the horses. Keep an eye on Riley until we get back."

"I hid your guns in the loft 'fore the cowpokes got here," Riley said. "Was afraid the sheriff would come back for them."

"Good thinking, thanks," Rance said.

"How you goin' to know which way they went," Riley said.

"Your horses have a blacksmith mark?" B.W. said. "Saw it on the shoe you was workin on when we came in."

"Yeah the horses I sold them have the marked shoes on."

"Tommy, keep an eye on Riley while we get supplies" Rance said. "We'll hurry."

Tommy nodded.

"What ya'll doin' in Traversville anyway?" Riley asked. "Where did that money come from?"

"It's a long story," Tommy said. "You goin' to be alright?"

"I think so now," Riley said.

Rance and B.W. were back in less than thirty minutes, ready to go. They tied down the supplies on the horses and climbed aboard. Rance pitched Riley the envelope the sheriff gave him.

"Give this to Travers for us, Riley, and tell him no deal."

"Good luck," Riley said. "You're gonna need it."

23

B.W., Rance and Tommy had been gone for almost a week when Julie and Fannie arrived in Traversville with Mitchell.

They rented a room at the Ferguson boarding house. The proprietor assumed Fannie was Julie's servant and allowed her to stay.

The morning after their arrival, Julie asked if the three had been to the boarding house and was told they were there over a week ago, was unacceptable, and had left.

Julie left Mitchell with Fannie and walked to the livery stable. Riley was feeding horses when Julie came in. He took off his hat and walked up to her. "Can I help you, ma'am?" he asked.

"Was looking for a one-armed man, an Indian and a boy ridin' together," she said. "Figured they would bed their horses here."

"Why you want to know," Riley said, remembering speaking out of turn about them before.

"Come a long way to find them."

"They was here, but I don't know where they are now. Supposed to be coming back."

"You know where they were headed? I was raised with the one-armed man, his name is Rance Allison."

"Yeah, that's him. Guess it would be alright to tell you. They went after two men that stole some money from them."

"How much money?"

"Don't know, but they had a suitcase full of it."

"First I heard of that. You know Robert Travers or Booker Church?"

"Yes ma'am. Mr. Travers owns the railroad and Booker works for him. Your friends got cross ways with Mr. Travers and they're gonna have to deal with him and Booker if they come back."

"You got a buggy I can rent?" Julie asked.

"Yes ma'am, dollar-fifty a day. I'll feed and water the horse. Need a five-dollar deposit. Pay the rest when you done with him."

"Get it ready for me, please."

"Yes ma'am." Riley picked up the tong of surrey and pulled it away from the wall, then grabbed a chair and carried it to her. "Have a seat miss...?"

"Julie Stryker," she said and sat down.

"Okay, Miss Julie, my name's Riley Jones. I'll go get the horse and harness, be right back."

The sound of hoof beats behind her caused her to stand up and turn around, there was a thin little man sitting on a paint horse with two pearl-handled pistols on his hips and fancy black and red boots stuck in the stirrups. He took off his black Stetson and placed his hand on the saddle horn and leaned forward.

"I'm Booker Church," he said, "I work for Mr. Travers. You the lady been askin' round about them no-goods came in from Virginia with the boy?"

"None of your business, mister."

"Afraid it is," he said. "They were threatening Mr. Travers. Can't let them do that without paying for it."

"Like you did Alice Woodson?"

"Don't know nothin' about that," he said and put his hat back on his head.

"Got a witness was there when you shot her down and ran out of town like an egg-sucking dog."

"I'd be careful what I said if I was you, lady," Booker said.

"Thank goodness you're not."

Riley came in with the horse in harness, stopped when he saw Church, then led the horse up to the buggy and began harnessing him.

"What you doin' here, Booker," he said, putting the bridle on the horse's head.

"Had a few questions for this pretty lady."

"Bout what?" Riley asked.

"My friends," Julie said.

"They're not here," Riley said.

"Found out they left town but didn't take Mr. Travers' deal. Just wanted to make sure they don't come back." Booker looked at Julie and flicked his tongue across his bottom lip like a snake.

Julie remembered what Cindy said. He did kind of remind her of a salamander.

"Don't know where they went and she don't either," Riley said.

"Better remember who runs this town, Riley."

"Best you get out of my livery stable."

"I'm done for now," Booker said, "but I'll be back. When I do,I may just have to kill you."

"What'll you do, shoot me in the back?"

"Don't have to. You're no match for me and you know it."

"Don't count on it," Riley said.

Booker tipped his hat toward Julie and smiled. "Good day, ma'am." He turned his horse around and rode out of the livery stable.

Riley was motionless for a few seconds watching Church ride away. "You know he's right. I ain't no match for him."

"He killed that boy's mama," Julie said.

"Better not talk about that round here," Riley said and started hooking the horse up to the buggy.

"I'm staying at the Ferguson boarding house. If you hear anything from them please let me know."

"I'll do that," Riley said and helped Julie up on the buggy seat and handed her the reins.

"Think I'll visit the sheriff, talk to him about Church," she said.

"Wouldn't do that, ma'am. Travers got the sheriff in his pocket, too. Just cause you more trouble."

Julie tapped the horse on the rump with the reins and rolled away.

24

B.W. kept tracking the shoe marks. He would lose the prints and pick them up again further along the trail until there was no doubt they were going straight west across Texas. They had to find shade in the middle of the day and pick up the trail again in the late afternoon. After a week of riding, they were about out of water. And that was much more important than the money at the moment.

Right before dark, they found a pool of water under a hanging rock from a spring and filled up the canteens and goat bags. They ate the last of the jerky and bedded down for the night.

"We're lucky we found water," Rance said. "May not be anymore if we keep goin.'"

"Yeah, gettin' too hot," B.W. said.

As the sun came up, they saw what looked like something burning a couple of miles away and rode toward it to see what it was. As they rode up, they could see two charred bodies tied to little mesquite trees, burned to the bone.

A large knife blade was laying in the ashes next to what was left of a leather boot. WP was etched into the blade.

"Well, we found Preston and Charlie. They got the money and horses," B.W. said. "Some bad hombres out here."

Suddenly, the sound of hoof beats filled the morning air. They saw at least ten riders silhouetted against the horizon as they rode across the top of a sloping hill nearby and dropped down in a gully.

They were coming after them. They could run or fight, but too many to survive either way.

"We'll have to make a stand long enough for Tommy to get away," Rance said.

"We know who burned Preston and Charlie and now they're comin' after us," B.W. said.

"Tommy, you ride out of here as fast as you can when the shootin' starts and don't look back,"

Rance said.

"No, I'm staying," Tommy said.

"No you're not," B.W. said. "I can hold them off long enough for you and the major to get away, no sense in all of us dying over my greed."

"You can't do it by yourself," Rance said. "It's goin' to take both of us shootin' as fast as we can to keep them pinned down long enough for him to get away."

"I can't run off like a coward," Tommy said.

"You're not, you're goin' because that's what you have to do. All three of us can't make it out of here," B.W. said.

"If you ever get the chance to see Julie, tell her what happened," Rance said. "I haven't been able to get her off my mind."

"Here," B.W. said and handed Tommy his tomahawk. "Won't be needing this anymore and I sure as hell don't want them to have it."

Tommy started crying. "Men don't cry," B.W. said.

Tommy wiped his eyes and took a deep breath. "I won't."

"Good." B.W. turned away from Tommy, wiping a tear from his eye.

"Take Buck," Rance said. "He's the fastest horse I ever rode."

"Don't slow down until you're ten miles from here," B.W. said.

"I got no place to go," Tommy said.

"You'll be alive," B.W. said. "That's all that matters."

The sound of a bullet ricocheted off a nearby rock.

"They're here," Rance said. "When we start shootin' go."

Tommy hugged Rance and B.W. "You'll always be with me," he said and climbed up on Buck.

Another bullet skipped off the top of a rock B.W. was behind and then two more.

"Go!" Rance yelled. They raised up from the rocks and started shooting as fast as they could cock the Henrys. Rance had become adept at firing the Henry fast by placing the stock in the crook of his left arm, squeezing the hand guard to hold it as he cocked the rifle with his right hand.

They stopped firing when Tommy was out of sight and dropped down behind the rocks again.

"I'm out of ammo," Rance said.

"Me too," B.W. said. "I think he got away."

"Been good knowin' you, B.W."

"You too, major."

"Sorry you didn't get to spend that money."

"Just as well," B.W. said. "I probably would've wound up in a place I shouldn't be."

Rance grinned. "That's how all this started."

"Yep," B.W. said.

"One good thing," Rance said, "at least Preston won't either."

"Still can't figure out how he knew we had that money," B.W. said.

"Was probably wishin' he never heard of it when those banditos caught up to him."

"Them Mexicans know how to kill a man almost as good as an Indian," B.W. said.

"Ain't going to let them have their fun with me, saving a round 'fore they get here," Rance said.

"Thinkin' the same thing," B.W. said. "They would skin me alive."

Rance nodded, checking the Navy Colt beside him.

They heard more hoof beats coming from a different direction saw a cloud of dust and heard rifle fire, but none of the rounds were coming their way.

They raised up and saw six riders riding down the jagged slope of the hill, firing rifles and handguns into the gully, then three more riders appeared, riding up from the ravine through the rocks, firing. They had the bandits in a crossfire. Several of the bandits tried to ride out but were cut down.

The sound of all the rifles was like the Fourth of July filling the air. It was over in minutes and the riders came together and galloped toward them.

As they got closer, the flickering sunlight bounced off the chest of some of the men and they saw Texas Ranger stars pinned on their chests.

"I'll be damned, they're lawmen," B.W. said.

The riders were close now. One of them was riding a little ahead of the rest on a big appaloosa. He threw up his hand and they reined their horses in and stopped. "Step out from behind those rocks with nothing in your hands," he said.

B.W. and Rance dropped the pistols, raised their hands and stepped out into the open.

The man on the appaloosa had his rifle lying across the pommel of his saddle with a Remington in his holster. He was tall in the saddle with a wrinkled weathered face, a droopy black mustache and a white Stetson covering his long, smoky gray shoulder-length hair.

A rider came galloping up to him.

"All of them are dead. What you want to do with the horses, captain?"

"Form a picket line and have two men lead them to the fort when we pull out," the captain said.

"Yes sir." The ranger spurred his horse and galloped back to the hill.

"I'm Captain John Unger," he said, looking at B.W. and Rance. "You can put your hands down. These are my men, the best guns in Texas."

"Don't doubt that," Rance said.

"Saw the shooting," Unger said. "What're you two doing out here?"

"Had a score to settle with two men, but those bandits got to them first and then came after us," B.W. said.

"You speak good English."

"Missionary school," B.W. said.

"What were ya'll chasing after the men for?" Unger asked.

"Kind of like to keep it to ourselves if you don't mind," B.W. said.

"Don't have a need to know now. You got a name?"

"Black Wind. Most people call me B.W."

"What tribe?"

"Cherokee."

"A bit out of your element, no?"

"Somewhat," B.W. said.

Unger turned to Rance. "And you?"

"Rance Allison. Thanks for savin' our asses."

"Truth is, we didn't know you were here. We're the only law around and don't get out here too often. That gang we just annihilated was some of the worst, mostly Mexican and Apaches. We been after them for months. You just happened to be here when we caught up with them. Guess I should thank you for slowing them down."

"We saw some of their work," B.W. said. "Caught the men we were chasing. When we found 'em they had plucked out their eyes, tied 'em to a tree and burned 'em alive."

"When was that?"

"Yesterday" B.W. said.

"You boys must not be Texan," Unger said. "Mostly nothing but renegades, Indians and snakes out in these parts. Most people just don't wander out this far."

"We're from Virginia," Rance said.

"You boys right with the law?"

"Hope so," Rance said.

"Maybe you better ride along with us to the fort," Unger said. "You can keep your guns."

"Out of ammo anyway," B.W. said.

"Mount up and stay close," Unger said.

Rance and B.W. gathered their guns and untied the horses. Rance climbed on the roan and B.W. on his black.

"How far we got to go, Captain?" Rance asked.

"About a day's ride to Fort Apache. We'll make camp when we get out of harm's way and ride on in tomorrow." He dropped his rifle in the sleeve and waved his hand for everyone to ride.

Before anyone moved they saw a rider come out of a thicket, riding like hell toward them.

"I got a bead on him, captain," one of the rangers said.

"Hold it till we know his intentions," Unger said.

The rider was closer now. "Don't shoot, he's with us," Rance said. "He's just a boy. We sent him away when we thought we were done for."

"Why in hell would you bring a boy out here?" Unger asked.

"An orphan we picked up on our way from Virginia."

"Still a dumb thing to do."

"We know that now," B.W. said.

Tommy rode up beside Rance, smiling, and pulled Buck to a stop and jumped off. "You're alive, major!"

"I think so," Rance said.

"Didn't know where to go. Hid in the brush over yonder and used your spyglass. Saw all the shootin' and spotted the Texas Ranger badges. You and B.W. ridin' with 'em, figured I better come back."

"Give me my tomahawk," B.W. said. Tommy handed him the tomahawk and hugged him.

"You a major?" Unger said, looking at Rance.

"Rebel major," Rance said.

"He went to West Point," Tommy said.

"Could use a well-trained officer if you're interested," Unger said.

"Got one hand, captain," Rance said.

"Can see that, but looks like it doesn't get in your way," he said and smiled. "What about you, B.W.?"

"Just plain old Indian," B.W. said.

"He's a lawyer," Tommy said.

"You're just full of information, ain't you," B.W. said to Tommy.

"That's a hard pill to swallow," Unger said and all the rangers in hearing distance laughed.

"My papers are in my saddle bags. Just don't use 'em much," B.W. said.

"We'll talk again later," Unger said. "Better get a move on now before we all get bushwhacked."

25

Rance and B.W. rode along side by side, their horses shaking their heads and stepping away from any of the ranger horses when they got too close.

"Guess it wasn't meant for us to have that money," B.W. said.

"Never did feel right about it anyway," Rance said.

"Didn't bother me."

"Kind of puts us back on track to take care of Tommy's problem."

"Don't think Travers is bluffin,' might have to kill him."

"What're we goin' to do if they try to put us in jail?" Tommy said.

"Run like hell if we get the chance," B.W. said. "I don't plan on spendin' the rest of my life in prison. Take off for California, won't matter out there."

"You talkin' bout me and the major, too?"

"If you want to come," B.W. said.

"Have to think on it," Tommy said. "Think the major might go back to Virginia. He keeps bringin' up Miss Julie a lot."

"That he does. Somethin' goin' on there, but none of our business," B.W. said.

Captain Unger rode up beside B.W. and Tommy. "You really a lawyer?" he said to B.W.

"I am," B.W. said. "Was supposed to represent the Cherokee nation but we had a misunderstanding about the war. I fought for the north, wasn't welcome back after that."

"Can see that happening," Unger said and let the appaloosa slow his pace.

Two hours later, they rode into a clump of trees, dismounted and posted lookouts, set a picket line for the horses and everyone found a place for their saddles to bed down. Rance walked up holding his saddle with his good hand and dropped it on the ground. B.W. and Tommy followed and dropped their saddles on the ground, too.

"Gonna fix some beans and coffee if you want some," Rance said. "After I gather some wood."

"I am kind of hungry," B.W. said. "Need some help with the wood?"

"I can do it. Still learnin' how to do things with one hand."

"I'll take some beans, don't want any coffee," Tommy said.

They broke camp the next morning and rode most of the day before reaching Fort Apache. They ate supper with the rangers and B.W. had Rance buy him a bottle of whiskey from the commissary because it was against regulations to sell whiskey to Indians.

Captain Unger came in the barracks and held up his hand and it got quiet.

"That was a hell of a job you did out there. Wanted you to know how proud I am of you," he said. "Anyone need some time off come see me." Everyone cheered. He stopped on his way out to talk to Rance and B.W.

"Been thinking on if you were chasing the two men instead of them chasing you," Unger said. "But I figured you was in the right. Gonna let sleeping dogs lie. Not gonna hold you up anymore. You can go when you want to. Would be a good idea to get back to a more civilized place with that boy. Tell the cook I said to give you a week's supplies."

"We're free to go?" B.W. asked.

"Yes," he said and walked out.

"What do you think, B W.?" Rance said. "What are we goin' to do?"

"Still want to find my mama's killer," Tommy said.

"Be working on a cold trail to find our way back," B.W. said.

"Want to try at least," Tommy said.

"Figured that," B.W. said.

"Not done with Travers either," Rance said.

"Still on that doin' something useful thing, huh?" B.W. said.

"Then it's settled," Rance said. "We're go back to Traversville."

"It is," B.W. said. "Now me and my whiskey are goin' to get reacquainted 'fore we do."

"Don't get too friendly, we got a long ride," Rance said.

"We'll just be kissing cousins," B.W. said, smiled and headed for his saddle bags.

26

Julie and Fannie had been in the boarding house for almost two weeks now with no word from anyone. She was spending her café money so fast there wouldn't be any left if she didn't make a decision soon on how she was going to make a living. She still had her looks and knew one way, but that wasn't going to happen if she had any other choices. Down deep inside she had hoped she could find Rance and he would be happy to see her and his son and they could become a family. Now that looked even less a possibility than ever.

Booker Church hadn't bothered her since the confrontation in the livery stable but she knew he would because of her big mouth. He could decide to silence her at any time or Travers decides for him.

Riley Jones was the only one she felt she could trust, but like he said, he was no match for Church. It might be best to catch the next train out to somewhere safe. She decided it was time to have a talk with Fannie.

She finished bathing Mitchell, dressed him and found Fannie on the back porch mending a fluffy pink dress.

She sat Mitchell down and gave him a corn dodger. "Don't remember seein' you in that dress," Julie said.

"Not mine, payin' me fifty cents to fix it. Got more to do."

Julie looked at the dress. "Pretty," she said then remembered why she was there. "It looks like we made the trip for nothing. I wanted to see how you felt about movin' on or goin' our separate ways. You have a right to choose your own path."

Fannie laid the dress down beside her and looked at Julie. "You know you never fooled anyone."

"What do you mean?" Julie asked.

"We all knew Mr. Rance was the love of your life, even if you didn't. Miss Paige was a good woman so I ain't faulting her, but I know how you feel and you have nothing to be ashamed of. Grew up in your house. Did what you did. Never felt like a slave though I knew I was. Got in a lot of fights over you with the other colored girls, ain't goin' to let none of that go to waste now. We wait, they'll come back," she said, picked up the dress and ran a needle through it.

"Never thought of you as a slave," Julie said.

"I know, why I'm still here."

"Wish I had your faith," Julie said. "If you will keep an eye on Mitchell, I need to take the horse over to the livery stable for Mr. Jones to feed."

"Here," Fannie said and handed Julie a derringer pistol out of her dress pocket.

"Where did you get that?"

"Had it for a long time," Fannie said. "Been keepin' it handy lately cause of that Church fella."

"Thanks." Julie took the pistol and stuck it in her hand bag.

As Julie drove up to the livery stable, two blonde-headed boys came out of the house next door and ran into the livery. Riley saw her and came over to her.

"Them your boys?" Julie asked.

"Come here, boys," Riley said, and the boys ran over beside Riley and looked up at Julie. "The oldest one is Riley Jr., he's ten, and the little one, William, is six. Say hello to Miss Julie, boys."

"Hello," they said in unison.

"Well hello," Julie said, "glad to meet you all. You look just like your papa."

They didn't say anything and looked at Riley. "Okay you can go play now," Riley said and the boys took off.

"I look forward to meeting your wife," Julie said.

Riley dropped his head and sighed. "Don't have one, a widower. Lydia died givin' birth to William."

"I'm so sorry, I didn't know."

"No reason you should. Thank you," he said. "Got some cool water in the pitcher if you want a drink while I take care of the horse. Gettin' hot early today."

"That's very kind of you," Julie said.

Riley helped her down from the buggy, brought a chair over for her to sit down, got her a glass of water and handed it to her. "Won't take long to feed and curry him. You need anything, holler."

"Thank you," she said and sat down with her glass of water and put her hand bag in her lap.

Riley filled the feed bag and hung it on the horse's head and walked back over to Julie. "Well, ain't seen hide nor hair of 'em. Been over two weeks. Would think they would be back by now if they was comin.'"

"Gonna wait a little while longer."

"Keep a watchful eye," Riley said. "Church is just plain mean. Would enjoy hurtin' you, and the sheriff, too. Round here it's Travers' way or no way. Got two boys to take care of, I do."

Riley didn't come straight out and say it but Julie knew he was telling her he couldn't help her. After Riley was done with the horse he helped her back up on the buggy and she drove out. A little ways down the street, Booker Church appeared on his paint and rode up next to her and grabbed the reins and stopped her horse.

"Mr. Travers thinks it time for you to leave and so do I."

"Well I don't, so let go of my horse." She placed her hand in her hand bag.

"Your friends are not coming back," Church said, "they know better."

"They'll be back."

Church smiled. "Be the biggest mistake they'll ever make."

"Let go of the reins."

"That pretty little nigger gal can stay, too, got plans for her."

"You can't buy and sell people anymore, Church."

"Might better keep a close eye on that boy of yours, could have an accident."

Julie jerked the reins and Church let go. "Get out of my way," she said, slamming the reins against the horse's backside and he trotted away, with Church leaning on his saddle horn, watching and grinning.

27

The sun was moving slowly across the Texas sky, showing no mercy for man nor beast.

"How long will it take us to get back to Traversville?" Tommy asked.

"Four, five days," B.W. said. "Can't diddle-daddle around out here, too many bad things can happen."

"Can get so hot you could fry an egg on a rock," Rance said. "You stay out in it long enough can fry your brain, too."

"Yeah, think we had enough for today," B.W. said. "I'm startin' to see cornbread walkin' across the ground."

"Those mesquite trees ahead are a good place to make camp," Rance said.

"Can we build a fire?" Tommy said.

"Better not," Rance said. "We're still in dangerous country."

"Got some canned beans and jerky," B.W. said.

"Oh goody," Tommy said, wrinkled up his nose and frowned.

"Beats goin' hungry," B.W. said.

They rode the horses up under a low-hanging limb, dismounted and unsaddled the horses and found a place to bed down under the shade of the trees, poured some water down the horses from a goat bag and tied them to a picket line. They strung a rope around their bed rolls to deter snakes coming too close. Sometimes it worked and sometimes it didn't.

"Kind of strange the way the weather is out here," B.W. said. "Hot as the hinges of hell durin' the day and cold at night." He took the whiskey bottle out of his saddle bags, took the cap off and took a swig. "Want a shot of whiskey, major?"

"Don't mind if I do," Rance said. "Help take the chill off." B.W. handed him the bottle.

Rance took a big drink and handed the bottle back to B.W.

"What about me," Tommy said. "I'm cold too."

"Sorry," B.W. said. "You don't get no more whiskey, might start to like it. Drink water, cover up with your blanket." B.W. screwed the cap back on the bottle and put it back in his saddle bags.

"You handlin' that whiskey real well now," Rance said.

"Got too much ridin' on me staying sober," B.W. said. "You and Tommy catch a wink, I'll take the first watch."

"So you'll know," Rance said, "wouldn't want anyone else at my back."

"Feel the same way," B.W. said.

Sounds they never heard in the daylight were loud in the dark every night. Prairie dogs barked, coyotes wailed and night birds chirped. The wind whistled through the little trees and shadows appeared from unknown creatures.

The next morning, they rode for hours across the barren prairie until a hot summer wind blew up a dust storm that made it impossible to go on.

They found a dry creek bed to block the wind and dust, tied their bandanas over the horses' eyes, stuck their hats in their saddle bags, put on their slickers and pulled them up over their heads and then huddled together against the creek bank and hung on to the horses' reins for dear life with both hands until the dust storm was gone.

By the time the storm was over, the heat was already on its way early the next morning.

They saw two riders coming toward them through the shimmering heat waves, too far away to tell who or what they were.

"What do you think?" B.W. said.

"Best to let 'em come to us," Rance said. "Use the creek bed for cover."

"I'll saddle the horses," Tommy said.

B.W. picked up the double-barrel, cracked the breach to make sure it was loaded and snapped the barrels shut.

"Tommy, you stay down and watch the horses," Rance said.

They waited for the riders to come into focus. There were two riders on one horse and a lone rider on the other, all of them wearing sombreros, sitting on big horn Mexican saddles with pistols stuck in their belts and the saddle boots filled with rifles.

They rode up to within earshot and Rance yelled, "That's close enough, what do you want?"

"Ah, gringos," the lone rider said. "Need your horses."

"Never gonna happen," Rance said.

The rider placed his hand on the butt of the Colt in his belt, the initials WP carved in the walnut handle. B.W. looked at Rance and he nodded.

The exhausted horses had their heads almost to the ground, sweat salt covering their chest ready to go down at any time, the one with the two riders in the worse shape.

The lone rider turned his horse sideways, dismounted, slid his rifle out of the sleeve and pointed at them over the horse's saddle. "Your horses now, señors, or you die."

The two riders on the other horse didn't move.

"No way," Rance said.

The horse with the two riders suddenly collapsed, dumping the riders off over his head to the ground and fell over on his side, dead. The two riders jumped up and ran to the dead horse for cover.

The lone rider's horse was frightened but too weak to run. He shook his head and staggered backwards, leaving the rider standing in the open.

He raised his rifle and Rance drew his Colt and put a bullet through his right eye and out the back of his head. Blood gushed out, covering his face and his dirty black shirt before he hit the ground.

The two riders stuck their heads up from behind the dead horse with their pistols in their hands and B. W pulled the triggers on both barrels of the twelve gauge and blew the guts out of the dead horse, and the faces off the two men, into buzzard meat.

The exhausted horse still on his feet stood there in a stupor, shaking, too tired to move from the spot.

"Looks like some of them did get away," B.W. said. "That was Preston's Colt he had."

"I saw it," Rance said. "Tommy, see if there's any water left in your goat bag and give it to that horse. I'll share mine with you."

Tommy grabbed the bag off his horse and shook it. "Some," he said and headed for the horse. The horse smelled the water and his ears went up. Tommy took the cap off, held his head back and poured what was left of the water in his mouth.

"I know what you're thinking, B.W. See if they have any of the money," Rance said. "I'll pick up the weapons."

B.W. sat the shotgun down and checked the saddle bags of the still-standing horse, nothing. He rolled the dead man over and searched him. He had twenty or thirty dollars in gold coins in his pockets.

"Not sure I want to do this one," he said, looking at the splattered horse's guts and what was left of the bloody faces of the two men.

"Suit yourself," Rance said.

B.W. frowned and pulled the saddle bags off the dead horse, blood and guts dripping from them. "Same as the other, empty," he said and quickly dropped the saddle bags. The two men had about the same amount of coins in their pockets. No more than a hundred dollars between all of them.

"Not much," B.W. said. "Nothin' to say to say it came from the robbery."

"Not surprised," Rance said. "Unger and his boys probably got the money off the dead."

"You don't want me to bury them, do you?" B.W. asked.

"Nope, we'll take the weapons and there won't be nothin' left but the saddles by sundown."

"You're learnin,' major. In time you might even be realistic," B.W. said. "Wasn't goin' to anyway."

Rance gave him a smirk, didn't say anything.

"We're not goin' to leave the horse are we?" Tommy said.

"No," Rance said. "Coyotes would have him in an hour. Unsaddle him."

"Good saddle," Tommy said.

"Don't need it," Rance said. "Get him some oats."

They gathered up their things and rode away.

Further down the trail B.W. pulled up his horse and looked at the surroundings. "Getting into some territory I remember on the way out," B.W. said. "That water hole we came by shouldn't be more than two or three miles from here."

B.W. kept turning back and forth in his saddle. "Yep, this is right," he said.

"Hope it's still got water in it," Rance said, as an afterthought.

In the distance behind them they could see the buzzards gathering over the dead.

At high noon on the fourth day, they were sitting on their horses under the shade of a big cider on a ridge overlooking Traversville, Tommy hanging on to the desperado horse.

"You were right, B.W., four days and we're here. Maybe you really are an Indian," Rance said.

Tommy smiled. "I knew he was right all along," he said.

"Of course you did," B.W. said and smiled. "You have a plan, major, or do we make one up as we go?"

"We'll go to the livery first and go from there."

"Then you don't have a plan," B.W. said.

"Not exactly," Rance said.

"Think Riley will be alright with us being in his livery stable?" B.W. said.

"Hope so. Don't have any other place to go," Rance said.

"I hate my Pa," Tommy said.

"Hate is a powerful thing boy," B.W. said. "Can keep a man from seein' the truth."

"Let's go find out what the truth is." Rance spurred his horse and took off, B.W. and Tommy right behind him.

Riley Jones was having supper in the livery with his two boys when they rode into the stable and dismounted.

Riley dropped a chicken leg onto his plate and stood up. The boys took a quick look and went right on eating the fried chicken.

"Well I'll be damned," Riley said. "You did come back."

"Told you," B.W. said.

"You get the money?"

"Nope," Rance said, "someone beat us to it and roasted the culprits we were after."

"Indians," Riley said.

"Mixed." Rance said. "Looks like you're doing okay," and pointed at the fried chicken.

"Miss Julie brought that over for the boys and I horned in on it."

"Julie," Rance said, surprised.

"Your friend, Julie Stryker. Thought you would be back all along. I had my doubts."

"Where is she?" Rance asked.

"Stayin' at the boarding house with that colored girl and the boy."

"What boy?" Rance said.

"Not sure, best you go talk to her," Riley said.

"I'll do that," he said, placed his foot in the stirrup and pulled himself up on Buck with his good hand by the saddle horn and rode away.

B.W. and Tommy watched Rance ride away

"Saw Fannie with a little boy, thought it was hers," Tommy said. "Come to think of it, he was kinda white lookin.'"

"Boy's white," Riley said, "about three or four."

"I'll be," B.W. said. "Guess we'll know all about it when the major gets back."

"Want some chicken? Got plenty. Miss Julie brought enough to feed twenty people," Riley said.

Riley's oldest boy stopped eating long enough to give a testimonial. "It's really good," Riley Junior said and went back to eating.

B.W. looked at Tommy, he smiled and licked his lips. "Thanks," B W. said. "Don't mind if we do. Been a while since we had a good meal. Was afraid we might have worn out our welcome last time."

"Nope. You need a place to bed down you can stay here," Riley said. "Might have to watch out for Travers and his bunch. They been pickin' on Miss Julie, tryin' to get her to leave town. She told me Travers' main gun hand, Booker Church, killed Tommy's mama. They don't want her telling anybody else, don't think they know she told me or they would be comin' for me, too."

"Where is this Church guy?" Tommy asked, opening up his saddle bags for the Navy Colt. "I'm goin' to kill him."

"Slow down, boy," B.W. said. "We need to know more about this first. No need runnin' off half-cocked."

"Don't care 'bout nothing else," Tommy said. "If he killed my mama, I'm goin' to kill him. The sooner the better."

"He might not want to be dead," B.W. said. "You think of that? He sees a gun, you're the one that will be dead. Calm down and let's wait for the major to get back and go from there."

"Better be soon," Tommy said.

"Eat some chicken and wait," B.W. said. "You can think better on a full stomach."

28

Rance rode up to the hitching post at the boarding house and dismounted, tied Buck and walked up to the door and knocked.

The pretty lady he had talked to before opened the door, holding the white cat.

"You Rance Allison?" she said.

"Yes ma'am," he said and took off his hat. "Is Julie Stryker staying here?"

"Yes, she spoke of you. Told her you had been here. That arm kind of makes you stand out. She's on the back porch. Follow the hall until you come to the screen door, that's the porch." She stepped back for him to come in, closed the door and walked away with the cat.

Rance hung his hat on the rack beside the door and walked down the hall and opened the screen door. Julie was sitting on a swing, Mitchell on the floor holding a toy horse.

"Julie," he said. "What...what are you doing here?"

She looked at Rance and stood up on wobbly legs. It took her a moment to find her voice. "Waitin' for you," she said.

"How did you know where I was?"

"A friend of Tommy's mama told me."

"Whose boy is that?" Rance asked, pointing at the child on the floor.

"He's yours, Rance," she said, her eyes getting moist. "His name's Mitchell."

"Mine!?...This is my son?" He stared at the little boy on the floor, his mouth open in disbelief.

"Should have told you a long time ago, was afraid you wouldn't believe me."

"Why should I now?"

"You think I would have come all this way if he wasn't?"

"Don't know," Rance said. "We spent one night together greivin' over Paige and my daughter and somehow wound up together. How could that happen?"

"It only takes once at the right time," she said.

"Unbelievable."

"Yeah that's what I thought," she said. "But there he is. You're the only one. He's yours."

"You should have told me 'fore I left Milberg."

"I know that now," she said. "A lot changed after you left. Colonel Hitch thought I was a bad influence on the locals and thought you were plannin' on startin' another war and I was in on it. He demanded I sell out and leave. Told him I would if he dropped the charges against you, he did and I left to find you."

"That's the craziest thing I ever heard," Rance said.

"That's what I thought," she said. "Riley told me 'bout the money and what the men looked like."

"Preston and Charlie, they wound up dead, and someone else got the money."

"Where did you get it?"

"We stumbled on to it," he said. "Left by bank robbers."

"A lot?" she asked.

"Twenty-thousand dollars. I'm still in shock over the boy."

"I wouldn't lie to you," she said.

"I believe you. I'm just trying to get a handle on everything. How long have you been here?"

"Since right after you took off after Preston. A prostitute from Whiskey Gulch came to see me. She worked with Tommy's mama, that's how I knew where to find you. She said she spent the night with a man named Booker Church that confessed when he was drunk to killing Tommy's mama. He works for Travers. Church knows I know and has been stalkin' me. I been expectin' him to shoot us at any time."

"This guy have two pearl-handled pistols and fancy boots?" Rance asked.

"He does," she said.

"That's the man Tommy saw the day his mama was murdered runnin' from her room."

"I'm sorry I didn't tell you 'bout Mitchell," she said and sat down in the swing, placed her head in her hands and began to cry. Mitchell jumped up and ran over to her, giving Rance the evil eye.

"Leave my mommy alone," he said with a devilish look.

Rance didn't know what to say and sat down beside her, Mitchell trying to get in her lap. She picked him up and brushed the tears from her face.

"I have a secret, too," Rance said and put his arm around her. Mitchell pushed it off.

"That night we spent together was more than you knew. I haven't been able to get you out of my mind since. One of the reasons I came back to Milberg was to see you. I thought about stayin' but I decided you didn't need a cripple and moved on."

"It doesn't matter 'bout your arm," she said. "Paige was buried 'fore we bedded together. Do you want us or not?"

"I do," he said.

The screen door opened and the land lady poked her head in. "Everything all right in here?"

"Yes," Julie said, "I think so."

Rance looked at Mitchell. "I have a son," he said and held out his arms for Mitchel. He looked at Rance's missing hand and started crying.

"Didn't mean to frighten him."

"He'll be all right," Julie said.

The screen door opened again and it was Fannie. She stopped in her tracks when she saw Rance.

"Well Lordy me, Mr. Allison, I told Julie you would come back."

"She did," Julie said. "I was ready to give up."

"Thanks, Fannie, for believing," he said.

"Julie tell you the trouble we're havin?'"

"Yes," Rance said. "B.W. and Tommy are at Riley's stable. Think we should join them as soon as possible."

"I'll get our things together," Fannie said. "Mitchell, you come with me. You can help me pack."

Mitchell looked at Rance suspiciously. "I want to stay with you, mama," he said.

"It's okay, baby, go with Fannie, I'll be there soon."

He slid off the swing, eyeing Rance and took Fannie's hand. She opened the screen door and led him away.

Rance placed his hand in hers. She threw both arms around him and pressed her lips to his and they kissed passionately.

"I'm very happy to find out I have a son."

"You've made me very happy."

"We've got a lot of catchin' up to do but we better get to the stable before some of Travers' men show up here," Rance said.

29

B.W. was sitting on a bench with a pile of chicken bones on a plate on the ground beside the bench, Riley gathering up the pots and pans, his two boys and Tommy washing them. Julie drove her buggy in the livery stable with three trunks on the back, Fannie and Mitchell on the buggy seat beside her and Rance on Buck.

Tommy walked over to the buggy. He stared at Mitchell then Rance. "Well, we know who his daddy is."

Julie blushed and Rance grinned.

"Dead ringer," B.W. said.

"Is, ain't he?" Rance said and climbed down off of Buck and held out his hand for Mitchell.

Mitchell scooted up close to his mama. "It's alright, Mitchell, he's your papa," she said.

Mitchell looked at his mama, then Rance, and shook his head no. Everyone laughed.

"Looks like he's got his concerns," B.W. said with a big smile.

Rance took Fannie's hand and helped her down, then Julie, Mitchell sitting on the seat.

"See, it's okay," Rance said and held out his hand to him and he slid over on the seat away from him.

"Maybe you better get him down, Julie. Looks like I got a lot to make up for." Julie held out her arms and Mitchell slid back over on the seat and jumped into her arms and she sat him down.

"Looks like our problems are getting bigger," B.W. said.

"Yeah, hell of a surprise. Better keep a lookout for Travers and figure out what we're goin' to do. Julie's changed my thinkin', got to take care of her and the baby now. Don't tell Tommy yet, but Julie said a whore that worked with Tommy's mama knew who killed her and it's that guy Tommy saw, and he's here."

"He already knows, Riley told him," B.W. said. "Been havin' a hard time keepin' him under control."

Rance nodded and noticed Tommy had disappeared. "Where'd Tommy go?"

"Was here a minute ago...oh no," B.W. said, shaking his head. He checked Tommy's saddle bags. The Colt was gone. "That crazy kid has gone lookin' for Church."

"Riley, you know where Church might be this time of day?" Rance asked.

"Most likely killin' somebody or in Big Sally's Saloon."

"How many gun hands Travers got?" B.W. asked Riley.

"The sheriff, maybe two or three bodyguards that stay with him all the time," Riley said. "A lot more with the railroad men but most of them wouldn't care whether he got killed or not. Church is the main one, the others more like bullies than gun hands. Kill you, though, if they get the chance. You take down Church first, the rest might give it up. Keep an eye on Church's left hand. Most people assume a man's right-handed and watch the right hand. That split-second gives him an advantage and then you're dead."

"We'll remember that," Rance said.

"Stay with the women and kids, Riley, me and B.W. have to find Church 'fore Tommy does," Rance said.

B.W. picked up his double-barrel and loaded it. Rance checked his extra Colt and the double-action and walked over to Julie and Mitchell. "Sorry, you know I have to do this," he said.

"Yeah, I know," she said. "I've waited a long time, so come back to me."

"I plan to. If, for some reason I don't, head for Austin and find the sheriff and tell him 'bout Church and what went on here."

Julie nodded, kissed him and whispered in his ear, "I love you."

"I love you too," he said and returned the kiss and squatted down and looked at Mitchell. "Could I have a hug if it's alright with mommy?" he asked.

Mitchell looked up at Julie. She nodded yes and he took a step toward Rance and hugged his neck and Rance kissed him on the cheek.

"Bye son," he said and stood up. "Fannie, take care of them for me."

"I will, I surely will," she said. "You take care of yourself and that big Indian. I think me and him will have to have a long talk when you get back," she said and smiled at B.W.

B.W. smiled back at Fannie and blew her a kiss. "Got to come back now," he said. "You ready, major?"

"Yes," Rance said. "Lock the doors, Riley."

Riley nodded, they walked out on the street and Riley closed the doors behind them.

"You know there's a very good chance we won't come back," B.W. said.

"I do," Rance said, "but you have to do what you have to do. We got the boy into this, we have to get him out."

"We do. It might change Travers mind some, too."

"B.W., I think you had the right idea to start with. Let's go kill that sonofabitch."

30

A door with Travers Southern Railway painted on it across the street from Big Sally's Saloon opened and Church walked out, fancy guns, boots and all. Then Robert Travers, with his white Stetson on and a black string tie around the collar of his starched white shirt.

Rance nudged B.W. in the alley and they watched Church and Travers cross the street and go in Big Sally's Saloon. Rance and B.W. stepped back out on the street and Tommy suddenly appeared and ran into Big Sally's, the Colt in his hand, before they could call out to him.

"Looks like it's goin' to be now or never," Rance said and they followed in after him.

Church and Travers were at the bar, their backs to Tommy, who was standing in the middle of the floor with the Colt pointed at Church. Church and Travers looked at them in the mirror behind the bar, Big Sally looking puzzled by it all. The men and whores in the saloon began to ease away toward the swinging doors except for a little whore not much bigger than Tommy that crouched down behind the piano.

"What the hell's goin' on here?" Big Sally asked.

"Church murdered the boy's mama," Rance said. "Used to work here, Alice Woodson."

"Did You kill his mama, Church?" Big Sally said.

"She was a no-good, money-stealin' whore," Church said to Big Sally.

Tommy cocked the hammer on the Colt.

Travers turned around slowly. "You a back-shooter boy?" he said. "That what you taught him, Allison?"

Tommy looked at B.W. and Rance in the mirror. "Ya'll go away, this is my fight," he said.

"You don't want to do this," Rance said. "Give me the gun."

"I'm goin' to kill that weasel."

"Put the gun down, boy, 'fore it's too late," Travers said.

Church hadn't moved, was staring at them in the mirror.

"That's what it'll be if'n he don't drop that gun," Church said to the mirror and picked up his whiskey glass, took a slow swallow and sat it gently back down on the bar.

"What do you care? She was a whore," Travers said and two men got up from their chairs at a table and walked over beside Travers, both big and ugly. They looked like they could chew nails and shit horseshoes.

"Get out of here, boy," Big Sally said. "He'll kill you." Church nodded yes, looking at Tommy in the mirror.

Big Sally reached down behind the bar and raised a shotgun up over the bar and pointed it at Church.

"You shoot that boy, you're dead too," Big Sally said. "Get out of my saloon and don't ever come back, all of you."

In one swift motion, Church wheeled, drew his left pearl-handled pistol and put a bullet between Big Sally's eyes before he knew what was happening. Sally fell backwards, pulling the triggers of the shotgun in a death grip, blowing a hole in the ceiling as he fell. Ricocheting buckshot and debris crashed against the big long mirror, smashing it to pieces. Tommy fired, hitting Church in his left shoulder and he dropped his pistol.

Travers crouched down in front of the bar with his hands over his head. The two men beside him reached for their guns and B.W. turned the shotgun loose on them and the buckshot went through them like a screen door, blowing the windows of the saloon out behind them. Church went for his right pistol. Rance put two holes in his left shirt pocket, about an inch apart, with his double action Colt before Church could clear leather. Church stared at Rance in disbelief, belched up his whiskey and slid down the bar to the floor, the longhorn steers on the side of his boots in full view.

The sheriff came running in, guns blazing, bullets buzzing by B.W.'s head like bumblebees. B.W. hurled the tomahawk across the room at the sheriff, planting it deep into his skull and blood squirted up like a fountain as he fell to his knees, the pistol spinning off his limp fingers and hitting the floor the same time he did.

Travers tossed his gun out on the floor and yelled, "I'm unarmed! Don't shoot!" and stood up next to the two disemboweled men on the floor with his hands over his head.

Out of the corner of his eye, Rance saw someone move and turned, ready to fire. A middle-aged man wearing a floppy straw hat, overalls and clodhopper boots was standing against the wall, his hands in the air. "Don't shoot," he said. "Got nothing to do with this, couldn't get out."

B.W. reloaded the shotgun and Rance walked up beside Tommy. "Give me the gun," he said and Tommy handed him the Colt.

"The Yankees goin' to hang you for this," Travers said.

"You're the one needs hangin' you chicken-livered bastard." B.W. sat the shotgun on the bar and poured himself a shot of whiskey, picked up the glass, looked at it and sat it back down hard on the bar. "Enough," he said.

Travers yelled something incoherent, reached inside his coat and pulled a two-barrel derringer and fired at B.W., hitting him in the head and side. B.W. staggered to the floor, the Colt falling out of his belt as he hit the floor.

Tommy reached down and picked up B.W.'s Colt and pointed it at Travers.

"No," B.W. said. He jerked the Colt out of Tommy's hand and shot Travers four times before he could fall.

"There goes the railroad," B.W. said and passed out.

Rance kneeled down beside B.W. and checked his breathing. "You got a doctor in this town?" Rance asked the man against the wall.

"Yes," he said, keeping his hands in the air.

"Go get him," Rance said. "Hurry!"

The man bolted for the door and out of the saloon. The people that were still in the bar were hugging the floor. Rance could see people standing outside the saloon, looking in as the swinging doors flew open.

"Is he gonna die?" Tommy asked.

"Don't know," Rance said. "Got to stop the bleedin.'"

The little whore came out from behind the piano and over to B.W. "Let me see," she said. "Use to take care of two brothers after battles." She stuck out a leg and ripped a piece of her petticoat off, folded it, picked up the bottle of whiskey on the bar, soaked the cloth in it and squatted down beside B.W. She placed the cloth in the wound and pressed her hands on it.

Less than five minutes later, a little gray-haired man carrying a doctor's bag came in with the sodbuster and saw B.W. on the floor with the little whore pressing the cloth on the wound.

"What the hell?" the doctor asked, looking around at all the dead men.

"Think he's the only one alive," Rance said.

"There's a bullet in his side," she said and stood up.

The doctor nodded. "Name's Meeks," he said and started working on B.W. "Looks like it missed the kidneys but it's goin' to have to come out. The head wound's not serious, more like a punch that just knocked him out."

"Thought so," she said, looking down at B.W.

"What's your name, lady?" Rance asked.

"They call me Little Sugar, real name's Maggie Pruitt. Heard what you said about the boy's mama. 'Fore my time but nothing Church did surprised me. Did some bad things to me, too, said he'd kill me if I told anyone."

"Thanks for your help, Maggie," Rance said.

"You're welcome. Thanks for killin' that bastard." Rance didn't say anything and just nodded he understood what she meant.

"Gotta go pack, no work here anymore," she said, walked by Church, spit on him, climbed the stairs to a room and went in.

"The bleeding is under control thanks to Little Sugar. Let's get him to my office," Doc Meeks said.

Rance looked at the man standing against the wall. "You just volunteered," Rance said to the sodbuster. "Think I can hold his legs with my arms, you get his upper body. Tommy, bring his hat and guns."

"What about the tomahawk?" Tommy asked.

Rance looked at the tomahawk in the sheriff's head. "In a good place where it is."

Most of the people in town had emptied out into the street and were watching as Rance and the sodbuster carried B.W. across the street to the doctor's office.

"Thanks," Rance said to the sodbuster as they laid B.W. on the bed.

"Wait in the other room," Doc Meeks said, rushing them out and closing the door.

"Thanks for what ya did back there," the sodbuster said. "I'm glad ya'll killed them no-goods."

"Better go 'fore the Yankees show up," Rance said and the man left.

"Tommy, I think it's okay to go to the livery," Rance said. "Go tell them what happened."

"I don't want to leave B.W."

"I know, but I'm sure they heard the gunfire and need to know we're still alive. Tell them to stay there for now. I'll keep a close watch on him till you get back."

"Alright, I'll be right back," Tommy said.

"It's okay, go ahead," Rance said and Tommy took off.

Doc Meeks came out of the back room wiping his hands on a towel. "Got the bullet out," he said. "He's out right now. Needs rest. Don't think it did any permanent damage, though. If you got a place to take him I think you should. Gonna be more trouble."

The front door swung open and a tall stout-looking man dressed in a Union officer's uniform with captain bars on his collar and a nervous look on his face was standing in the doorway, his saber in one hand and a Navy Colt in the other. Two soldiers were standing behind him with carbines.

"Drop your guns, mister," the captain said. Rance dropped the Colt from his belt and unbuckled his gun belt and let it fall to the floor.

Two soldiers walked in from the back room. "There's a wounded Indian on a bed back there, Captain Welch. I left Private Ferguson to watch him."

"You know anything bout this, doc?" Welch asked.

"No, got there after it was all over. Been treatin' the Indian."

"Looks like a war zone over there, bodies everywhere," Welch said. "You a Yank or a Reb?" he asked, looking at Rance's arm.

"Neither now, captain. The war's over."

"That Indian part of your band?" Welch said.

"He's my friend, yeah," Rance said.

"He killed Travers, didn't he?"

"He did, after Travers pulled a gun on him."

"What's your name?" Welch asked.

"Rance Allison."

The doctor's office door came open again and a broad-shouldered man with intense brown eyes and a neatly trimmed

THE LAST GOOD DAY

black beard walked in with silver leafs on the collar of his shirt. All the soldiers snapped to attention and saluted.

He returned the salute and stared at Rance, rubbed his chin. "Wasn't you at West Point? Class of fifty-eight?"

"Sure was," Rance said. "Thought I remembered you. William Smith, right? We had some Calvary tactics classes together."

Colonel Smith nodded. "Rance Allison, been a while."

"Was a different world back then," Rance said.

"That it was," Smith said, "Heard you switched sides."

"I resigned my commission. Union troops murdered my wife and baby, my Pa and ma for no reason."

"There's a wounded Indian in the back room that helped him kill those men," Welch said.

"On your West Point word of honor, Rance, who started it?" Smith asked.

"They did," Rance said. "Church shot the bartender and Travers' men drew down on us and the sheriff came in firing at us."

"One of the witnesses said a boy was in there holding a gun on Church," Welch said.

"That right?" Smith said to Rance.

"Yes sir," Rance said. "Travers is the boy's pa, had Church murder his mama. Would have killed the boy if he got to him to keep him from getting a share of his railroad."

"And you know that for a fact," Colonel Smith said.

"I do," Rance said.

"Don't cotton to a man that would kill a woman and a kid," Smith said.

"She was a whore," Welch said.

"Doesn't matter. You got anyone that says different from what he said, Captain Welch?"

"No sir."

"Make me out a report to that effect and I'll sign it, send it to the adjutant," Smith said.

"What!?" Welch said. "They should be tried for murder. They killed a lawman and the only southerner we could trust to help run this town."

"Captain, I'm in command here. You're free to go, Rance. Sorry 'bout your family," Colonel Smith said. "Might be best if you move on as soon as you can."

"We'll do that," Rance said.

Colonel Smith nodded. "Captain, I want that report by ten in the morning."

"Yes sir."

Colonel Smith turned to the door, a soldier opened it, and he walked out.

"Can we have our guns back now?" Rance asked.

"This is not the last of this," Welch said. "Give him his weapons, sergeant."

Rance took his guns and the soldiers left.

"Okay if I check on B.W., doc?"

"Sure," he said.

Rance walked into the back room and placed a hand on B.W.'s shoulder and he opened his eyes.

"That you, Rance?"

"First time you ever called me by my given name."

"Figured it was time. A man worth ridin' with should be called by his name."

"How you feelin?'"

"Like I got a hoe handle stuck up my ass."

"Not too far off. You been shot in the abdomen. Doc got the bullet out."

"I still got my pecker?"

"I'll let you check that," Rance said.

"My own damn fault, should have been watchin' that sonofabitch," B.W. said.

"That was a good thing you did, not letting Tommy kill him."

"He needed killin' but Tommy didn't need it on his conscience," B.W. said. "Don't think he's goin' to get any of that railroad since I killed his pa."

"No matter. He didn't want it anyway, was us pushing it."

"Tommy gonna be okay?" B.W. asked.

"Worried 'bout you. Sent him to the livery stable to tell 'em we're still alive. Turns out the commanding officer here is an old friend of mine. We're free to go but that won't stop anybody from killin' us if they get the chance. Got to go get a wagon to get you out of here."

"Tell that Fannie girl I'm still kickin.'"

"I'll do that," Rance said. "Doc, keep an eye on him."

31

When Rance walked in the livery stable there were smiles all around. Julie ran to him and threw her arms around him. "You're alive!" she said.

"I am. B.W.'s wounded but I think he's goin' to be alright," Rance said.

"Where is he?" Julie asked.

"At the doctor's office. Needs some transportation, can't sit a horse."

"I'll get a wagon," Riley said and headed for the corral.

Fannie walked up holding Mitchell. "B.W. goin' to make it?" she asked.

"Think so," Rance said. "He said to tell you he's still kickin.'"

Fannie smiled and Rance held out his arms for Mitchell, but he turned away and hugged Fannie.

"He'll take to you," Julie said. "Take a little time, is all."

"Where'd you get the name Mitchell?" Rance asked.

"Just liked it," Julie said. "Wasn't sure you would want him named after you."

Rance held out his arms again for Mitchell and he grabbed Fannie around the neck.

Riley came back into the livery stable with two horses pulling a flatbed wagon and jumped down off the seat. "This oughta do," he said.

"I'll go get him." Rance stepped on the wagon wheel axle and sat down on the seat.

"I'm goin' too, "Tommy said and climbed up on the wagon beside Rance.

"Giddy up," Rance said. They rode by Big Sally's Saloon and Rance stopped the wagon in front of Doctor Meek's office, tied the horses to the hitching post and he and Tommy jumped down from the wagon and went in.

"How's he doin?'" Rance asked.

"Better than I expected. Main thing is to make sure he doesn't start bleeding again. Normally, I wouldn't recommend he be moved yet, except them vultures may come back. I'll help you put him in the wagon."

Riley met Rance at the door and held the horses while Rance and Tommy got off the wagon and everyone checked on B.W. in the wagon.

"Was worried bout you," Tommy said.

"We all were," Julie said.

"Thanks. Sorry 'bout your pa," B.W. said. "Didn't have a choice."

"He had it comin,'" Tommy said.

"Maybe so, but that don't make me feel any better 'bout it," B.W. said.

"You did what you had to do," Rance said. "I think its okay for you to have a nip, want me to get the whiskey?"

"No, don't have that cravin' like I did," B.W. said. "Chief Drowning Bear liked whiskey so much he drank himself into a trance when he was sixty years old and everyone thought he was dead. He woke up the next day and announced he had been to the spirit world and talked to friends and god and was sent back from the dead inspired to quit drinking. From that day on he forbade anyone else in the tribe to drink for the rest of his life. I had that same dream when I was lying on that bed in the doctor's office. Scared the hell out of me."

"Want somethin to eat?" Fannie asked.

"Got any of those biscuits?" B.W. said.

"No, but I can make some."

"I sure do love those biscuits," B.W. said. "Don't think I want the whiskey this time. The cravin's gone."

"I'll bring you some biscuits when they're ready," Fannie said.

"That'll be good, you can join me."

"I'll do that," Fannie said, smiled and walked away.

Tommy sat down in the back of the wagon beside B.W. "Wanted to tell you I been thinkin' about goin' to West Point, if I can learn enough. The major said he'll help me till I get in. Don't think I would make a very good lawyer."

"Me neither," B.W. said.

"Then it's alright with you?" Tommy said looking at B.W.

"Hell yeah, you might be president one of these days."

"What are you goin' to do, B.W.?" Tommy said.

"Don't know, what 'bout you, Rance?"

"Julie got a letter from Jack's wife some time back, used to own the eatery. She said there's a valley in California that looks like Shenandoah with land free for the takin.' Thinkin' about goin' there and startin' a new life. Why don't you come with us?"

Fannie walked up with the biscuits and sat the plate down beside B.W. He looked up at Fannie and smiled. "Fannie girl, would you marry me and go to California?"

"What?" she said, looking sideways at B.W. "I barely know you."

"No better way to get acquainted than to be married," B.W. said.

"I heard that," Julie said, a big grin on her face. "You must really like those biscuits."

"Well?" B.W. said, looking at Fannie.

"You're serious?"

"I am. Time I started my own family."

Fannie stood there staring at B.W., studying him like it was the first time she ever saw him. "You really mean it?" she asked.

"I do," B.W. said.

"I must be crazy but I'll do it," Fannie said. "I will marry you."

"And go to California?" B.W. said.

"Yes," she said, pushed the plate of biscuits over and slid in beside B.W. and they embraced and kissed.

Julie poked Rance in the ribs and pointed toward B.W. and Fannie.

"Okay, as soon as we can find a preacher," he said.

The sound of hoof beats interrupted the moment and Rance walked over to the closed doors and peeked through the cracks. "We got company and it's the wrong kind," Rance said. "It's that Captain Welch with soldiers and civilians, maybe twenty or more."

B.W. reached out and picked up his shotgun. "Open the doors," he said. "We can't outgun 'em, but maybe we can scare the hell out of 'em."

"Julie, you and Fannie get the kids and get up in the loft," Rance said. "You too, Tommy."

Fannie slid out of the wagon and her and Julie gathered up the kids and climbed up in the hay loft, Tommy following.

"Riley, we kind of boxed you into this," Rance said. "You know this means you got to leave too if we get out of this alive."

"It's alright, I ain't takin' any more from them," Riley said. "Better to be dead than a coward."

Riley and Rance loaded their shotguns, opened the doors and stood by the wagon with B.W. stretched out in the wagon, the barrel of his shotgun on the sideboard pointed toward the doors as Welch and the rest rode up. Welch held up his hand and they all stopped in front of the open doors.

"Came to arrest you for murder," Welch said.

"The colonel said we were free to go," Rance said.

"He was called away to Washington. I'm in command till he gets back, and that may be a month, gonna hang you 'fore then."

"You're gonna have to come and get us," B.W. said and cocked the hammers on the shotgun.

"You think you can hold off all of us?" Welch asked.

"No," B.W. said. "But I can damn sure kill you first."

"And while he's doing that, me and Riley are goin' to pick out who else goes with him." Rance said.

"You ready to die, captain?" B.W. said. "Cause I am. We may all have already seen our last good day."

"You're crazy," Welch said.

"Probably," B.W. said. "Make your play if you're goin' to. I'm gettin' an itchy trigger finger."

Several of the riders began to move away from Welch and two turned their horses around and galloped away.

"These scatterguns can take a lot of you with us. Better think about that 'fore you start shootin,'" B.W. said.

"Let 'em be, captain," one of the riders said. "I ain't dyin' for Travers."

"Good advice," Rance said.

Welch sat on his horse real still, looking at the shotgun B.W. had trained on him, sweat popping out on his face. He licked his lips, raised his left arm slowly and wiped the sweat from his forehead with the back of his hand. "Okay," he said. "No sense anybody dyin' today. You got till morning to be out of town."

"Thought you might see it that way," B.W. said, eyeing Welch, his finger on the triggers of the shotgun.

"Let's go," Welch said and they turned their horses around and rode away.

"Could tell he was goin' to back down by the look in his eyes," B.W. said.

"What if he didn't?" Rance asked.

"Guess we all would be dead, including him."

"I truly believe you could scare the hell out of the devil."

"Give it a try if I had to," B.W. said. "Where's Fannie? I think she said yes."

"I did," she said and climbed down from the loft and got back in the wagon with B.W. He laid the shotgun down and picked up a biscuit. "Tommy, do me a favor. Get me a cup of water."

"Sure," Tommy said, climbed down from the loft, dipped a cup in the water bucket and took it to B.W.

"Thanks," he said. "I'm getting married. I got to make a fast recovery."

"Me too," Rance said, smiling at Julie.

"We got to go to the capital in Austin and file the papers for Tommy's inheritance of Travers' property. The colonel gave us a clean bill of health to do it. Wait for an answer," B.W. said. " If he gets it, he's going to be a rich young man. He don't even owe me a fee for doing it"

"How long will it take," Rance said.

"Don't know," B.W. said. "Rather do it personally so I know it's officially on file. If he wins he'll never have to worry 'bout money again."

"Do we have to come back to Texas?" Rance said.

"No, just make sure it's in the works. Don't think he would want to come back. Too much pain left here. Can sell it for millions."

"They can send it to the address Julie has in California," Rance said.

"Good, load me up and head for Austin," B.W. said.

Rance and Riley loaded B.W. on the wagon and they sat his rocker in beside him. Julie sat Mitchell next to her on the wagon seat. Fannie helped the boys climb up beside Mitchell. They watched Tommy carve his name in the livery stable door. He could write his name now. That was a good start, Rance thought.

Rance took Julie's Colt and handed it to Tommy.

"You have earned the right to carry this on you," Rance said. "You know when and how to use it."

B.W. raised up from the wagon. "You damn sure have," he said.

"Thank you," Tommy said and stuck the gun in his belt.

"Take us to Austin, Julie," B.W. said and Julie snapped the reins. The horses did a stutter step and started pulling the wagon.

Two days later, they arrived in Austin with everything they had. They dropped everyone but B.W. off at the church to get ready for the weddings. Rance and Riley carried B.W. from the wagon in his rocking chair inside the capitol building to the estate office where he filed the papers for the inheritance. They carried him back to the wagon, then from the wagon to the church. They had to sit down in a pew to catch their breath.

"Who the hell needs a horse," B.W. said, smiling like the Cheshire Cat at Rance and Riley.

They had a double wedding ceremony, Tommy was best man for both. After the wedding, they loaded up the wagon. B.W. had the double-barrel beside him. They tied B.W.'s horse to the back of the wagon. Julie and Fannie took turns reining the wagon. The Riley boys played with Mitchell and kept him entertained. Tommy and Riley rode along each side of the wagon, with Rance riding point as they headed for California, each with thoughts of their next big adventure.

THE END

ABOUT THE AUTHOR

John L. Lansdale was born and raised in east Texas. He is married to the love of his life Mary. They have four children. He is a retired Army reserve psychological operations officer and a combat veteran that served three tours in Vietnam with numerous medals and awards. He is a graduate of a Texas police academy and a state certified peace officer. He is an inventor, country music songwriter, performer and television programmer. He produced the television special "Ladies of Country Music" and several other programs. He goes back to the Sun Record days and was introduced to Elvis Presley by Mary on their first date when Elvis was a seventeen-year-old student at Humes High School in Memphis and a ticket-taker at Loew's State Theater.

John has produced a variety of albums and music videos for country artists in Nashville along with songs for movies, with one as recently as 2018 titled "Tremble" for an upcoming film. He has hosted his own radio shows and won awards for radio and television commercials. He was a writer and editor for a business newspaper. He has worked as a comic book writer for Tales from the Crypt, IDW, Grave Tales, Cemetery Dance and many more. He co-authored *Shadows West* and *Hell's Bounty* with his brother Joe. He is the author of *Slow Bullet*, the four-part Mecana detective series, *Long Walk Home*, *Zombie Gold* and several others.

John's novel *Slow Bullet* was reviewed by Publishers Weekly as a must read page-turner with constant action and compared his work to that of popular 1950s author Mickey Spillane. The novel *Long Walk Home* was a finalist in the fiction category for the National Indie Excellence Awards. The novel *Zombie Gold* received great reviews including a Booklist review that praised it as a superb story with characters that came alive. *Kissing the Devil* received praise a pulp novella. All titles are still in print with new ones on the way.

John was recently inducted into the Gladewater Museum. His motto is: ***Never Give Up***.

THE MECANA SERIES
by JOHN L. LANSDALE

HORSE OF A DIFFERENT COLOR – Book #1

Dallas PD Detective Thomas Mecana is on the hunt for a serial killer terrorizing the Lone Star State. Joining him is Darcie Connors, a young officer working her first murder case. With hard work, and some luck, Mecana and his partner discover a most-unusual serial killer case with murder in its very genes.

WHEN THE NIGHT BIRD SINGS – Book #2

Detectives Thomas Mecana and Darcie Connors are on the trail of a new suspect. With an ever-growing suspect list, Mecana must toe the line between friend and foe. Each action leaves them sitting in the crosshairs of danger. One wrong move could mean the end.

TWISTED JUSTICE – Book #3

Dallas Homicide Detective Sunday Verves is looking into the suspicious deaths of local drug runners when she discovers a potential suspect that hits too close to home. When the trail leads her south of the border, she enlists some old friends to track down the suspects.

THE BOX – Book #4

Detective Thomas Mecana and the gang get back together for another case. Mecana soon finds the case is bringing back old evidence. This horror-filled novel brings the Mecana Series full-circle to where it all began.

STAY CONNECTED
WITH
BOOKVOICE PUBLISHING
AND
JOHN L. LANSDALE

www.bookvoicepublishing.com

CPSIA information can be obtained
at www.ICGtesting.com
Printed in the USA
BVHW030350130621
609420BV00009B/80/J

9 781949 381245